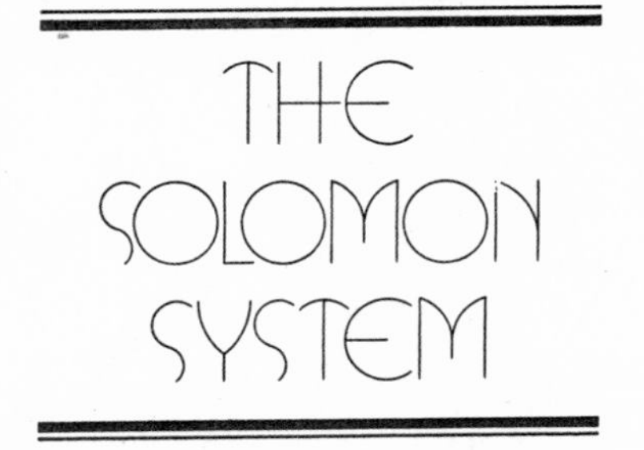

BOOKS BY PHYLLIS REYNOLDS NAYLOR

Witch's Sister
Witch Water
The Witch Herself
Walking Through the Dark
How I Came to Be a Writer
How Lazy Can You Get?
Eddie, Incorporated
All Because I'm Older
Shadows on the Wall
Faces in the Water
Footprints at the Window
The Boy With the Helium Head
A String of Chances
The Solomon System

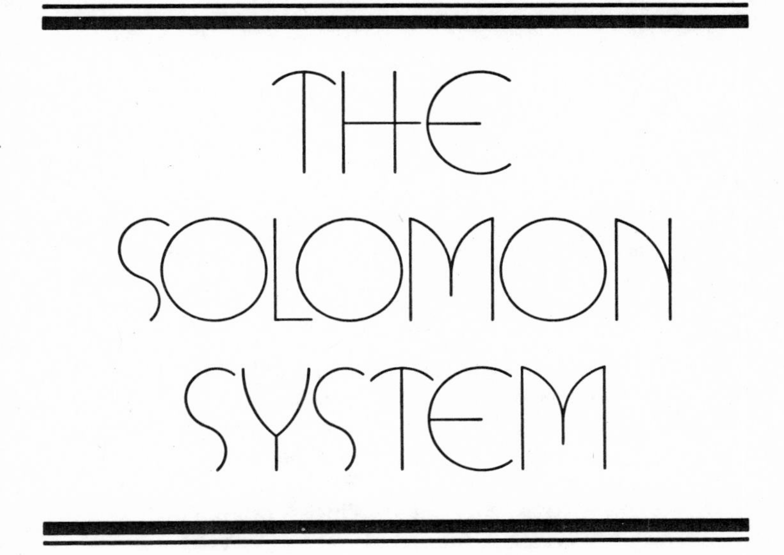

Phyllis Reynolds Naylor

Atheneum 1984 New York

LIBRARY OF CONGRESS CATALOGING IN PUBLICATION DATA

Naylor, Phyllis Reynolds.
The Solomon system.

SUMMARY: Thirteen-year-old Ted and his older brother, Nory, have always been a team until the summer family problems make them reevaluate their relationship and their expectations of each other.
[1. Brothers—Fiction. 2. Family problems—Fiction] I. Title.
PZ7.N24So 1983 [Fic] 83-2661
ISBN 0-689-30991-0

Published simultaneously in Canada by
McClelland & Stewart, Ltd.
Composition by American Book-Stratford Graphics,
Brattleboro, Vermont
Printed and bound
by Fairfield Graphics, Fairfield, Pennsylvania
Designed by Mary Ahern
First Printing July 1983
Second Printing July 1984

To the Monday-night group—Larry Callen, Helen Jacob, Gloria Kamen, Marguerite Murray, Gene Namovicz, and Peggy Thomson—with love and appreciation

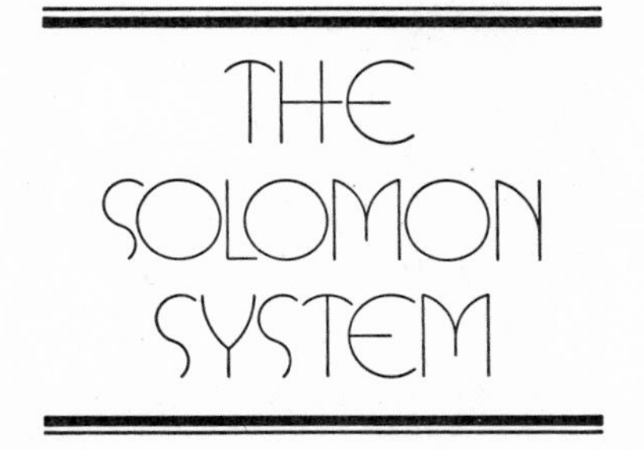
THE
SOLOMON
SYSTEM

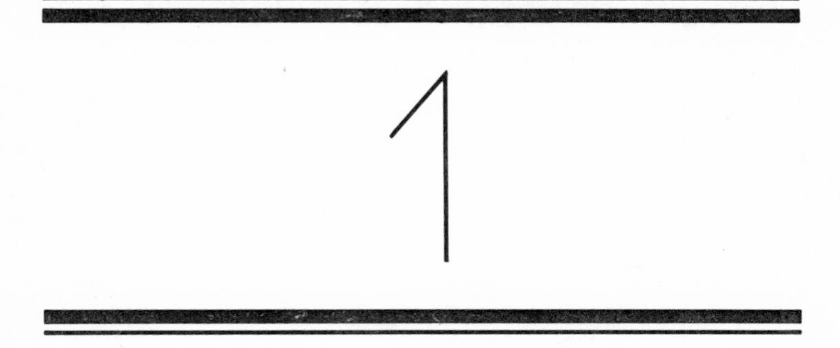

"Ted, tell your father that dinner's ready."

I moved my electronic blob to one corner of the screen, where he smushed an invader. I listened for sounds from the den. Sometimes Dad got right up and came. I knew he'd heard.

The electronic blob turned on the guys behind him and smushed them, too.

"Ted!" came Mom's voice again.

I took my feet off the hassock and let the blob have one more go at it before I switched the game off. Still no sound from the den. I got up and slouched across the room.

"Dad," I said from the doorway. "Dinner."

"Tell her I'm coming," he said.

"He's coming," I said to Mom. I was a blinking messenger service, that's what.

We look alike, Dad and I. Both of us are tall, both are skinny—even our noses—and we both have dark hair. Only I'm thirteen and Dad's forty-one, and he's going bald, and I'm not. Nory, my brother, worries about body hair. He'll be sixteen next month, and he hardly has any hair on his legs. He says if he doesn't get hair on his chest he can live with it, but if he doesn't get hair on his legs, he'll kill himself.

"Hey, Nory," I told him once, "some guys don't even have legs, and they manage."

"Hair's different," Nory said.

That's the one thing about Nory I don't understand. We agree on everything else.

I don't know when it was I started not liking dinnertime at our house. The last couple years, anyway.

Mom and Nory were already eating when I got there. Mom and Nory look alike—same stubby noses, square faces, gray eyes, curly hair. Mom, though, wears glasses—huge round lenses tinted pink. They kept sliding down her nose, and every so often she pushed them back up with one finger.

There was cauliflower, which Dad hates, on the table. At least three times a week, we have cauliflower. Dad sat down and sort of shoved the dish away, banging it against the water pitcher. Then he helped himself to the beef brisket.

"How's driver's ed?" he said to Nory.

Conversations at our table go from Dad to Nory, Dad to me; Mom to Nory, Mom to me. If Nory and I don't stick around for dessert, Dad and Mom don't stay at the table either.

"Well," Nory answered, "mostly we've been driving around Kensington. Mr. Mott says he'll have us on the beltway next week."

"The beltway!" said Mom. "Good grief!"

"I think you can handle it," Dad said to Nory.

Then it was my turn. As soon as one of us gets over a question, the other gets one. I guess our parents figure that as long as they're talking to us, they don't have to talk to each other.

"Well, Ted, how was your day?" Mom asked.

I always try to have something ready. Sometimes I even plan it before I get up in the morning—try to think of a story that will make the whole family laugh. But this time I forgot. So my mind ticked off all the things that had happened at school, and finally I said, "I saw a tapeworm this morning. Mrs. Kuhn took it out of a jar and spread it on the table. It was nineteen feet long."

"Good grief!" Mom said again.

"And Mrs. Kuhn had you measure it and count the segments, right?" Nory laughed.

"Right."

"Must be the same one she had when I was in her class. 'Charlie,' we called him."

"It's really interesting," I said. "The head attaches itself to the wall of your intestine and the body keeps growing and makes eggs. And when the embryos escape from the eggs, they burrow—"

"Okay, Ted," Mom said.

But I wasn't through yet. ". . . they burrow through the intestine and make their way into muscles and—"

"Theodore!" said Mom, unsmiling.

"All right," I said. "But that's why you're supposed to thoroughly cook your meat."

Dad looked down at his beef brisket.

Cleo was scratching at the back screen, her three pups tumbling around her. She smelled the brisket. I remembered that Cleo had worms once and was about to ask what kind they were, but decided I'd better not.

The kitchen was quiet with only the clink of forks against the plates, and Cleo's whining. If we were a *Brady Bunch* rerun, I was thinking, somebody would say something clever about now, and the mother and father would laugh. If this was the *Little House on the Prairie,* the parents would look lovingly at each other as though wild horses couldn't pull them apart. But this was the Solomon family in Kensington, Maryland, and it was a toss-up whether Mom or Dad would leave the table first.

And then Mom said, "Someone's coming by after dinner to see the pups."

Part of me didn't want anyone taking the pups until they stopped being so cute and wobbly. The other part wanted someone to take them away before I got too attached to them. Nory and I didn't even name them this time, not when we knew they'd only be around for six or eight weeks.

"Someone going to buy them all?" Nory asked.

"I don't know. But we're not keeping any, remember. One dog around here is enough. Unless somebody *else* wants to take over for a change."

I knew Mom didn't mean Nory and me. We're good about giving Cleo baths and exercising her and everything. Mom meant somebody to drive Cleo back and forth to the vet's and remove her ticks and give her medicine when she got sick and clean up after her when she was *really* sick. Dad picked up his pie, took it into the den, and closed the door.

After dinner I fed Cleo and then went out on the front porch where Nory was standing, hands in his pockets. He was looking at Mr. Goldstein's Thunderbird and Mrs. Boyd's Impala parked across the street and at the empty space between them.

"I've got to learn to parallel park," he said.

Now the first thing you should know about Nory is he's not very practical. In the second place, he's sort of a klutz. He makes A's in history and algebra, but when it comes to mechanical ingenuity, Nory hasn't got any. Like the day he tried to get a ball off our roof and put the ladder through a window. And the time he put the handlebars of his bike on backwards.

"Nory," I told him, "just one little dent in that Impala and you'd have to mow fifty lawns to pay for it."

"How am I going to learn?" said Nory.

"I'll think of something," I told him.

I got two cardboard boxes and a couple of brooms. I stuck the brooms in the boxes, so the brooms would stand up, and set them in the street about eighteen feet apart. Dad told Nory he could practice if he stayed out in front, so Nory backed our Buick down the drive. Across the street, Mrs. Boyd stopped weeding and moved her Impala around the corner.

"You know what to do?" I asked Nory, coming up to the window.

"Yeah. Mr. Mott showed us a movie in class."

I stepped away from the car.

Nory let up on the clutch too soon and killed the motor. He started again, but this time pressed too hard on the gas. The left front fender swung out into the street and the Buick varoomed backwards, coming to rest sideways in the space, both rear wheels up against the curb.

"Well," I said to Nory, "you didn't knock down any brooms."

Nory tried again, but I could tell right away he wouldn't make it. He cut back in too sharply and moved the first broom a couple feet. Mr. Goldstein came out and pulled his Thunderbird in his driveway.

I tried to imagine Nory on the beltway between two Mack trucks. I tried to imagine him on Rockville Pike trying to cut into the left-hand lane. I tried to imagine him anywhere at all in Kensington trying to parallel park. Nory's face and neck had turned pink from the effort.

Dad came out on the porch and stood watching. Across the street, Mrs. Boyd stopped weeding again and was looking our way. Nory pulled up as close as he could to the broom without touching it. He had just started to back in when suddenly he pounded his foot on the brake, his eyes on the rear-view mirror.

I turned. There sat a girl on a bike, watching.

"Who's that?" I asked Nory.

"Some girl in the band," he said disgustedly. "Mickey Johnson."

"Hey," I called to her. "How about moving it?"

"Oh, sure." The girl in the red shorts backed up. Then she rested one foot against the curb and waited.

Nory took a deep breath. "I can't park with all these people looking," he said.

I stuck my head in the car window. "Nory," I told him, "this is your finest hour. If you can park it now, you can do anything."

I moved away from the window. "Keep it slow," I said. "Just inch it in."

The car began to move. The left front fender swung out and then curved back again. The right front fender merely tapped the broom box but didn't move it. The back wheels came within an inch of the curb but didn't scrape, and Nory was parked.

Dad gave him the OK sign and went inside. Mrs. Boyd returned to her weeding. Mickey Johnson pulled up alongside the Buick.

"Hey, that was real good!" she said. "When I get my learner's permit, you can teach me."

Nory gave her a small smile, and she rode away.

We worked for another half hour. I'd stand out in the street and signal, showing Nory how close he was to the broom box, and he'd practice pulling in next to the curb.

When Mr. Goldstein came out to check his

sprinkler, he called, "What's this? The Solomon System?"

It was an old joke. Mr. Goldstein used to say it when Nory and I hooked our sleds together and came down the hill side by side. He said it when we rigged up a bucket and pulley in the apple tree and one of us stayed at the top and picked while the other emptied apples out at the bottom. He was always kidding us because we did things together, the two Solomon brothers. But we always have. We like each other. We need each other, I guess.

Nory had just parked the Buick in our driveway again when a Toyota pulled up. A woman got out and said she'd seen our ad for a springer spaniel. We took her around to the back porch, and Cleo came over and licked her. Cleo's so dumb she can't even tell when somebody's about to walk off with her babies.

Mom came out with the breeding papers to show that the pups were pedigreed, and while she and the woman talked, Nory and I sat on the glider, petting Cleo, running our hands through her brown and white fur. She looked up at us with her mouth open, her tongue dripping saliva—dog-happy dumb.

Inside, the doorbell rang, and then we heard Dad's footsteps as he went to answer. A minute later he appeared on the back porch.

"Elaine, here are some more people to see the pups," he said pleasantly.

"Fine," Mom said. "Everyone loves a springer spaniel. They're so good-natured."

I watched my parents as they laughed and chatted with the people there on the porch. They gave their smiles to strangers and saved their silence for each other. I couldn't remember when it all began. Long before my bar mitzvah, I was sure of that. "Today I am a man," I said in temple, and Mom and Dad had seemed so proud and smiled so much that I thought maybe from then on things would be different. But the next day they were back to silences again, and I didn't feel like a man at all. I felt pretty scared, in fact; like maybe—with all the relatives gone—whatever had been waiting to happen would. I kept trying to think of something else to keep my parents busy, but a bar mitzvah's a hard act to follow.

"You can just tell they've been given a good home," a woman was saying now, stroking the pups. "They seem so happy."

I went upstairs and lay down in my bed. I could hear my parents' voices as they followed the people out to their cars and stood talking with them at the curb. Why couldn't they sound like that all the time? I mean, why couldn't they just *want* to get along with each other and then *do* it?

The phone rang and I answered from the upstairs hall. It was Grandma Rose.

"Ted?" she said. "So how goes everything?" She meant Mom and Dad.

"The same," I told her.

"Oy vey." Grandma sighed. And then, "You want I should come down?"

"Yes," I said. "What about tomorrow?"

"I'll catch the train at one and take the Metro from Washington," she told me. "Chin up."

I went down to the back porch. The fattest pup had been sold, as well as the one with the all-white head. I was hoping that someone would buy two, but the runt was left. He wobbled over to me, sniffing my shoe, and then leaned against my foot.

I knelt down and picked him up, holding him against my shirt, feeling his sandpaper tongue on my hand. I wondered what it was like to suddenly lose a brother and sister. Or what Cleo herself was feeling. I thought how unfair it was to say that dogs don't feel anything just because they can't talk.

The next day, a girl came by and bought the runt.

Nory and I are named after dead people. I'm named for my great-uncle Theodore, who died of hepatitis, and my cousin Everett, who got hit by a bus. Nory is named for my grandfather Norman, who fell down the stairs, and Grandfather Isaac, who died in his sleep. Theodore Everett Solomon and Norman Isaac Solomon, that's us. But you wouldn't believe Grandma Rose.

She was born Rose Myrtle Chapman in 1906. (She was named for her sister Myrtle, who died at birth, and her Aunt Rose, who died of pneumonia.) But when she married my grandfather, Norman Rose, her name became Rose Myrtle Rose, or Rose

Rose. I was thinking about that the other day. If you were writing a story about my grandmother, you could begin by saying, "It was morning, and Rose Rose rose."

Grandma Rose is Mom's mother. She lives in Baltimore in the same house where Grandpa Norman fell down the stairs. Every year, just before Passover, she cleans that house like it was infected or something—every room, every closet, every shelf. After she scours the stove and scrubs the refrigerator, she tapes up the cupboards so we can't eat anything but special foods on special dishes. In our house at Passover, we just buy a box of matzoh.

We all like Grandma Rose, even Dad. She can walk in a room where two people aren't speaking and get something going. They'll always talk to Grandma—laugh with her, even. And that's the way it was when she got to our place the next day.

"For gosh sake, there's Mother!" Mom said, looking out the window as a cab pulled up, and the next moment a little woman with bluish-white hair and an overnight bag was shoving a loaf of pumpernickel in my hands and hugging us all.

"You didn't let me know you were coming!" Mom half-scolded, carrying her bag up to the spare bedroom.

Grandma didn't say that I'd forgotten to tell them she'd called.

"I should tell you I want to visit my own daughter?" she asked. "You always told me my room was ready, so here I am."

That night, the conversation at our table went from Dad to Nory and Dad to me and Dad to Grandma Rose; Mom to Nory, Mom to me, Mom to Grandma Rose; and from Grandma to everyone else at the table.

"Some more chicken, Rose?" Dad asked, handing her the platter, but she waved it away. Grandma is always on a diet.

"I couldn't eat another bite," she said, and nibbled at the corn I'd left on my plate.

That's another thing about Grandma. She never nags Nory and me to eat.

"What's to worry?" she'll say if we don't finish all our scalloped potatoes. "You want fat boys, Elaine? Fat girls I can stand, but fat boys look like sausages. You want sons or sausages?"

We had been talking about Cleo and the pups, and Grandma told us a story about when Mom was two years old and the family had just bought a German shepherd.

"Lola, that was the dog's name," Grandma said. "Elaine was as jealous as she could be. She was used to being the pet of the family herself, and suddenly it was the dog her brothers wanted to play with. So one night, when the boys were fighting over whose turn it was to feed Lola, Elaine just put her own dish on the floor, got down on her hands and knees, and started to eat."

Nory and I yelped with laughter, and I was surprised to see Dad laughing, too. Mom blushed and smiled a little, and I was really glad that Grandma had come. Maybe things weren't so bad between my folks after all.

When dinner was over, Nory and I went to the high school to lift weights. Every summer, see, we go to this camp in Pennsylvania where there are all kinds of sports. Nory's got lots of strength in his arms, but mine still look like mop handles, so Nory takes me to the weight room to work out.

I liked being inside the high school. It's bigger than the junior high, and there are always things going on at night. On the way to the gym, we passed room 107, biology. Nory tried the door. When it opened, he said, "Come here, I want to show you something," and turned on the light.

There were charts along one wall illustrating the reproductive systems of fish, but Nory was taking the lid off a big container filled with plastic bags. He took out one and held it up. Inside, in some kind of liquid, was a little pink animal without any hair, its eyelids swollen shut.

"A fetal pig," said Nory. "We started dissecting them yesterday. Monday we have to find the gall bladders."

I winced.

Nory put the lid back on the container, and I followed him into the hall. Those fetal pigs bothered me. Maybe Cleo's pups would end up here. What did we know about the people who bought them? Maybe they took them for research. I didn't like it that we bred Cleo and then sold her litter to anyone who came along. I felt that we all should stay together as long as we could—Nory, me, Cleo, the pups . . . .

I did pretty well on the bench press. I only weigh a hundred and six pounds, but I got up to eighty on the press, five pounds better than last time.

"Good!" Nory said. "We'll have you lifting your own weight pretty soon. Try it again, and exhale while you push."

I began to lift, and the weight moved up. I could tell by the strain in my arms that I was doing better than I had before. I saw Nory smile and knew I'd passed eighty-five. I pushed with everything I had, aiming for ninety. *Whang.* My elbows gave out, and the weight came crashing down in the groove behind my head.

"Eighty-five!" Nory said. "Hey, Ted, you did all right!"

The soccer team came in to work out, so we had to leave, but I really felt great on the way home. I was thinking about the baseball games at camp, and how maybe I'd hit the ball further this year. It's a coed camp, see, and even though the girls don't play on the boys' teams, there's always a bunch of them watching. The only thing worse than striking out in front of your own team is striking out in front of a bunch of girls who are going to talk about you—how far you hit or how fast you ran or whether or not your undershorts were showing.

"Do you ever wish it was just a boys' camp?" I said aloud.

"Oh, I don't know," said Nory.

I glanced over. "What if Mickey Johnson ever showed up there?"

"Yuk," said Nory, and then I felt better. The thing about Nory is he never thinks these things through.

We came to the end of the field and took the path back to our street. Mom and Grandma Rose were sitting on the front porch. We could hear their voices as we came up. We must not have been making any noise, because they went right on talking in the darkness. We paused for a moment there by the rain spout.

"Sometimes," Mom was saying, "couples grow apart. Gene and I just aren't the same people we were when we married, that's all."

Grandma Rose has a habit of clicking her false teeth when she's thinking what to say next. Standing there in the dark I could hear the faint *click, click.*

"Okay, maybe you're different. That's so bad?" she said finally. "Identical twins you should be?"

Mom sighed. "There's only one thing we have in common anymore, Mother—only one thing we both care about a lot, and that's the boys."

That *really* scared me. It was as though Nory and I were the only glue holding my folks together. The one thing worse than feeling you can't do anything is the feeling that it's all up to you: you're responsible. I figured I'd just have to try harder.

Nory pulled at my arm, and we slipped around to the back. He went upstairs to do homework, but I hung around the door of the den. Dad was watching a baseball game on TV. He motioned me to come over, and when I sat down, he put one arm around my shoulder. I wondered if he knew what Mom was saying out on the porch.

I waited for a commercial, then said, "Dad, I don't think Mom's very happy."

At first I wasn't sure he'd heard me. It was a light beer commercial with Rodney Dangerfield, and Dad chuckled. But then he grew quiet. "What makes you think that?" he said.

It was a stupid thing to ask. I wanted to tell him I wasn't deaf and blind. Instead, the lump in my throat got bigger and I just shrugged.

Dad patted my shoulder.

"I know she's not," he said finally. "And I don't guess there's anything I can do about it."

I swallowed.

Dad didn't look at me—just kept patting my shoulder every once in a while, in a kind of rhythm. "Sometimes things don't turn out the way we wanted, Ted, and sometimes we're not even sure why."

The commercials were over, and Dad seemed caught up in the game again, so I slipped out from beneath his hand and went upstairs.

He hadn't got the point. I have to know where things are headed. I'm the one who watches the road map when we go on a trip while everyone else looks out the windows. I like to say, "Huntsville coming up, Dad, in exactly two and a half miles," and then see the sign for Huntsville. But suddenly here we were, on a trip without a map. I didn't know what was coming next, and I don't think my folks did either.

It was about two when I woke, and there were noises in the kitchen. Nory was sleeping soundly, lying half off his bed the way he does, so I didn't wake him. Besides, I knew who was down there.

I got up and went to the kitchen.

"In such a world, who can sleep?" Grandma said when she saw me. "I was just warming some milk. Sit down. Do you want some?"

I noticed that she had the cocoa out as well, but we have this understanding: I never mention her diet. When she saw my eye on the opened box of cookies, though, she added, "I'm just eating the broken pieces."

We both smiled.

I sat there at the table beside Grandma, watching my marshmallow melt in the cocoa. She had her hair down, and it hung about her shoulders like a thin white cape. Grandma's skin is always pink, even at two o'clock in the morning.

"I wish you'd come down every weekend," I told her.

She clicked her teeth. "Soon enough you'd be tired of me."

I shook my head.

"Oh, yes you would. The first few weeks? Hugs and kisses. By the end of three months, you wouldn't even come to the door."

"Is that what happened to Dad and Mom?" I asked. "They grew tired of each other?"

"You're asking me?" Grandma said. "I'm the answer-woman, maybe?" Then she fixed her eyes on me, and they looked very small without her bifocals. "What can I tell you? That's for them to know and us not to know, I guess. *Some* things may be wrong in this family, Ted, but not *everything* is wrong. You've got six more inches to grow, seventy pounds to gain, and four more years of school—college I'm not even counting. That's more than enough worries already."

It helped some to have my work laid out for me, to know that there were limits. I sat there until the marshmallow had turned to foam on top of my cocoa, and then I drank it down.

On school mornings, I set the clock radio exactly in time for the weather report so we'll know if it's snowing and the schools are closed, or it's so foggy we can't see, or there's a flood and cars are stranded on the parkway. Then we listen to the news to be sure we're not at war with anybody. Finally, I reach over and turn on some rock music for Nory, to soothe him while he examines his legs for any hair that might have grown up overnight.

Nory gets up first, though. He uses Old Spice deodorant in a push-up container. He smells like Uncle David, who even uses cologne. I don't know how Aunt Sheila can stand him. Nory says I'll embarrass myself some day if I'm sitting beside a girl and realize I stink, but when I asked him if I stink he said not yet.

On this particular morning, after Nory went in the bathroom, I remembered the picture I'd cut out of *Sports Illustrated* showing a tennis champion getting a trophy. I got out of bed, found the picture, and taped it to Nory's mirror. I always look for pictures of famous men who don't have much hair on their legs, and then I leave them around where Nory will find them. It's hard to find pictures of famous men without trousers.

"What's this?" Nory said when he came back. He pulled on his jeans and looked at the picture while he buckled his belt.

"Oh, that?" I yawned. "It's just the guy who won the singles tournament in West Germany, that's all."

"What's he doing on my dresser?"

"I sort of thought he looked like you."

"Him? You're nuts." Nory pulled on his socks.

I sat up on one elbow. "Well, I mean . . . your legs look alike."

"Our *legs?*" Nory still didn't get the point.

"Well, he doesn't have any hair on his either."

Nory stared at the picture. "He's blond, for Pete's sake! He probably has scads of hair. You just can't see it."

I got up and brushed my teeth. I wished we could trade worries for a while. I'd worry about body hair and he could worry about Mom and Dad. It's funny, but Nory and I don't talk much about them. We talk about everything else. He told me about that magazine he found once, and even showed me the pictures. And I told him about getting detention at school for starting a water fight. But talking about parents is different. Once you admit there's a problem, you can't pretend anymore that there isn't.

We eat breakfast in shifts. Dad's the first one out in the morning, because he has to catch the Metro at seven-thirty. He's a computer analyst for the government and works in Washington. Mom manages a travel agency over on Connecticut Avenue. So Dad eats first, then Mom and Nory, and I eat alone while Mom makes my lunch.

She looked awfully nice. She was wearing a summer dress in three shades of green.

"It's going to be downright hot today, Ted," she said. "You might want to reconsider and wear cut-offs."

She might as well have told me to go barefoot. Junior high is different from elementary. *Nobody* wears cut-offs until it's so hot your jeans stick to your legs.

"No, I'm okay," I told her.

"Do you want tuna salad or pastrami?" she asked, getting out the sandwich bread.

"Pastrami," I told her.

"Mustard or mayonnaise?"

"Uh . . . mustard."

"An orange or banana?"

"Orange."

"Chocolate chip or sugar cookies?"

"Chocolate chip."

"To go, or will you eat it here?"

We both laughed.

She was in a good mood, so I added, "You look real nice, Mom. Dad always liked you in that dress."

"Really?" said Mom, without expression.

I didn't push it any further. I was thinking about the stupid thing I did a couple years ago. I was worried because Dad hadn't given her a birthday present so I bought a card that said, "To my darling wife," and forged Dad's name. I copied it with carbon paper from his signature on a bank book, which was about the dumbest thing I ever did, because after the long syrupy verse on the inside, I signed it, "Eugene M. Solomon." To make it worse, I forgot that postage had gone up, and when the card arrived, Mom had to scrounge around for three cents.

I was still thinking about it when John Jennings sat down beside me on the bus. I don't know what it is, but there are some guys who, the more they try to be friends, the more you resist. There's nothing wrong with John. It's just that he's so predictable. I know that as soon as the bus stops at Saul Road, he's going to get on and say, "How you doing, Ted?" and if he can't sit beside me, he'll sit in front or behind, and then he'll hang over the back of the seat and talk.

"Hi, Ted, how you doing?" he said, sliding in beside me.

"How's yourself?" I said.

"I got some new stamps from Ceylon," he told me. "Want to come over this afternoon and see them?"

The problem with John's stamp collection is that he only collects birds. When a block of twenties came out, a bird for every state, John went nuts. He bought a whole sheet for his album and another to frame. Can you imagine having a guy for a friend who hangs postage stamps on his wall?

"Well, maybe some other time," I said to John. "I'm sort of busy tonight. I've got things to do with my brother."

"Okay," said John. "Some other time."

When I got off the bus that afternoon, I almost wished I'd gone home with John instead, because when I started down my street, there was this big gray dog named Brute. Every so often he jumps the fence, and there he stood, ears perked up, tail stiff, watching me come.

I crossed over to the other side, but I knew it wouldn't make any difference. The gray dog must own all the territory fifty feet out from his house in every direction, and he started barking when I was four houses away.

I read somewhere that you should approach a barking dog with your hands in plain sight so he can see you don't have a stick or something, and that you should stop and turn sideways and not look him in the eye.

Well, it doesn't work with Brute. I've tried putting my hands on top my head like a prisoner of war. I've tried standing sideways and telling him that my family was waiting for me at home and to please let me grow up to be a father, but he just keeps circling and snapping till the little old lady who owns him calls him in.

This time, when I was directly across the street from Brute, he charged. I immediately stopped and turned sideways, pretending I was examining a tree, but he kept leaping up, snapping at my sleeve.

And then, far down the street, I saw Nory on his bike. The thing about Nory is that you don't have to yell or anything. He just knows. And there he came, hunched up over the handle bars, picking up speed.

Suddenly the bicycle was right between Brute and me, and I hopped up on the crossbar. The dog wheeled around in confusion as Nory made a U-turn, and then we were careening back down the hill, whistling and shouting at the dumb dog, who ran another twenty feet and gave up. The Solomon System worked again.

"Stupid mutt," Nory said, as he leaned his bike against the house.

My heart was still pounding, but I managed to laugh. "Boy, did he look surprised when you rode up. He didn't know whose leg to go for first."

It wasn't really a rescue, see—just a joke on a dumb dog. I didn't have to tell Nory I was afraid. There are a lot of things we understand that we don't have to talk about.

Forms had come from camp for us to sign, so after dinner Nory and I spread them out on the dining room table. There were papers for the doctor to sign after we'd had our physicals, so that if we dropped dead in a soccer game, no one would sue. There were forms for Mom and Dad to sign, saying they wouldn't hold the camp responsible if we did something dumb, like stand up in a canoe. And there were forms that Nory and I had to fill out saying what sports we wanted to do most.

What's great about Camp Susquehannocks is that usually the same kids come back each summer. Nory and I started going when I was five and he was eight, and now that I'm thirteen, I'll be in the same bunkhouse with Nory and some other teen-agers. We could do all kinds of things together this year that we couldn't do before.

Nory's a waiter. You get to be a waiter when

you're fifteen. There's no pay, but you get lots of extra privileges, so everybody wants to make waiter. When you're seventeen, you can't be a camper anymore, but you might be hired as a bunk counselor, and you only have to pay half tuition. Bunk counselors get *lots* of privileges. After you graduate from college, you can be a full counselor.

I looked over the program. *Put a number beside each activity listed,* the instructions said, *with number one representing the sport that interests you most and number ten the one you care about least.*

I put one and two beside swimming and volleyball and nine and ten beside wrestling and football.

Dad came in and leaned over my chair.

"Well, how does the line-up look this year? They got anything new?"

"Street hockey," I told him. "Maybe I'll give it a try."

"Hey, they've got handball," he said, reading the program. "That's something I would have liked."

"It's so beautiful up there in those hills," said Mom from the kitchen. "I'm sure you boys are going to have a wonderful time."

An alarm went off inside me. I don't know what it was, but all of a sudden I felt they wanted us out of the way, that something was going to happen.

I looked across at Nory, but he was busy putting down his numbers. I didn't like the idea of being in Pennsylvania for six weeks, not knowing what was going on back here. I thought suddenly of something Mom had said years ago when John Jennings' folks split up. I asked her if that would ever happen to her and Dad and she just said, "That's something we'd have to think about a long time." Maybe the long time was up. And then I remembered Grandma Rose. I knew she'd keep an eye on things if I asked.

The phone rang, and I answered.

"Is Nory there?" It was a girl's voice.

"Nory," I said, going back in the dining room. "Some girl."

Nory frowned and went in the front hall. I could see him from where I was sitting. He stood with one arm stiffly at his side.

"Yeah?" There was a long silence. He stood on his right foot and put his left up on the stool. Then he put his left foot down and his right foot up on the stool.

"Huh-uh," he said finally. Another long silence.

"That's okay," he said at last. "Yeah, sure." And hung up.

"Who was *that?*" I asked when he came back to the table.

He grabbed his pencil and began writing again.

"Mickey," he mumbled.

"Mickey Johnson?" I looked at him. "What did *she* want?"

"Wanted to know if she had to have a learner's permit before she can take driver's ed. She's signed up for it this summer."

I laughed. "Boy, can you see Mickey trying to parallel park?"

Nory laughed, too. "That would be something," he said.

I'm not sure why I was laughing. I don't even know Mickey Johnson. But I was glad that she was registered for summer school and wouldn't somehow show up at Camp Susquehannocks. The girls at our camp are different. They're like sisters, almost, and we kid around a lot. It's like going to a family reunion and seeing a bunch of cousins. I was pretty sure that Nory felt the same way.

On the last day of school, my junior high really goes wild. A lot of kids don't bother to come at all. The rest of us wear something crazy, like plaid shorts and polka dot ties, or hats with ears on them. Last year even the principal came in argyle socks and red suspenders.

The teachers try to entertain us. They show movies or read Edgar Allan Poe. Sometimes they put us to work cleaning out their supply cupboards, and then we sort of disappear and go see what the other rooms are doing.

This year, I was debating whether to go to school in long johns and an Ohio State tee shirt or skip and go play video games at the mall. To tell the truth, I've never skipped before, and I thought I ought to warn Mom, in case she took that morning off and saw me go in the arcade.

"Where's Mom?" I asked Dad, watching him soap the hubcaps of the Buick. He had the hose propped up on the roof of the car, and trickles of water were running down the windows and doors.

"I don't know," he said, and went on scrubbing.

I went back inside and finally found Mom in the den, sorting through papers.

"These files are a mess," she said. "Haven't been cleaned out in years."

I leaned against the doorframe. "Hardly anyone's going to school tomorrow," I told her. "There's not much point in it."

She cast me a suspicious glance. "If there wasn't any point in it, they wouldn't be holding classes, would they?"

"They've got to get in a certain number of days, Mom, that's all. I think the teachers are actually glad when we don't show up, so they can get some work done."

"Ha!" said Mom.

"Well, I might skip," I told her.

She frowned. "I don't know about that. Let someone else make the decisions around here. Go check with your father."

I went back outside.

"Absolutely nobody's going to school tomorrow," I told him. "I'd probably be the only one on the bus. I think I'll skip."

"Wait a minute," Dad said. "What does your mother think about that?"

"She thinks whatever *you* think!" I yelped in exasperation.

"Well, if nobody else is going . . ." Dad said finally, and let it drop. Then he asked, "What's your mother doing?"

Ted, the Spy.

"Sorting through stuff," I told him.

"In the den?"

"Yeah."

Dad frowned and went on rubbing a fender.

As it turned out, I went to school after all. It was too hot for long johns, so I just put on the Ohio State tee shirt over a pair of Hawaiian print shorts and some long red knee socks. I figured I'd probably have more fun there than at the mall. John Jennings had his clothes on backwards, and another guy was wearing a raincoat; every so often he'd flash it open to show the Batman undershorts he was wearing, and the girls would scream.

The real reason I went to school was that Mr. Emory said he might give away his old map of the world. Teachers give away lots of worn-out stuff on the last day of school. But when I got to the history room, someone else had asked for it first. Mr. Emory gave me a booklet about presidents, published by a cereal company, but I'd really wanted that map. I decided to go home and see if Nory was around. As I passed the science room, I went in to say good-by to Mrs. Kuhn.

I think fate sent me there. I think it just grabbed me by the elbow and marched me over to her desk, because there in the waste basket was a glass jar. And in the jar was "Charlie."

I stared.

"Hi, Ted," Mrs. Kuhn said when she saw me. She was fussing with plants by the window. "Big plans for the summer?"

"Camp," I told her.

"That's nice."

"Mrs. Kuhn, about this tapeworm. . . ."

She turned around. "Do you want it? I'm afraid Charlie's almost finished. He's been around so long he's coming apart. I ordered a new one for next year."

"I can *have* it?"

"Certainly, but I can't imagine what you'd do with him."

I couldn't either. All I knew was that I was probably the only kid in Kensington with a tapeworm in a jar.

"Have a good summer, Mrs. Kuhn," I said,

and went home holding that jar like it was the queen's jewels. At least it would be something to talk about at the table.

When I came to dinner that evening, though, Mom was slinging plates on the table as if she were dealing cards, and Dad's spoon went skidding off the other side. Dad just left it on the floor. I knew right away that it wasn't the time to tell about the guy in the raincoat and the Batman underwear, or what I found in Mrs. Kuhn's wastebasket. Whatever the argument was about this time, it must have been a whopper, because Mom and Dad were even too angry to talk to us.

We were like robots, the way our hands moved to our mouths and back again. At some point I heard Dad sigh, a private sigh. He was chewing as though the food didn't have any taste, and it suddenly occurred to me that Mom wasn't the only one who was unhappy.

What hurts, what really hurts, is that I love both of my parents. If somebody held a gun to my head and told me to choose between Mom and Dad, I'd let them shoot me. But it sure gets awkward sometimes. Sometimes I just want to yell at them, "Oh, grow up!" Can you imagine a thirteen-year-old kid telling his folks to grow up? They didn't always act this way, though, and that hurts most of all—the remembering. Like the time we stopped by the road and bought a muskmelon, and the farmer cut it for us. We sat close together in the grass, eating that melon and laughing—and when we got home we planted the seeds. That's the kind of remembering that hurts.

Now I felt trapped by their silence and looked over at Nory. He was dividing everything on his plate in half, the way he does when he wants to get away fast. That's the way Nory is when he's upset; he just eats half and starves himself. Not me. I stay there and pig out, because as long as I'm there, my folks won't fight. *Ted, the referee.* Sometimes Mom will look at me and say, "Aren't you through, yet?" and I'll say, "No, I think I'll just have some more Jello." Anything to stay at the table. It's what goes on behind my back that scares me most.

Well, the silence got deeper, and I had the horrible feeling I might jump up and do something wild. Just grab hold of the table and push it over, dishes and all. I really have weird thoughts sometimes, but just when I was sure I had things under control, I belched.

It wasn't an ordinary belch, but a loud, long, thumb-your-nose kind that started in low and then ricochetted around the kitchen. I didn't mean to do it, but I didn't stop it, either. It just sort of hung there in the air. Nory stared at me.

"Theodore, leave the table," Mom said.

"An apology will do," Dad told me.

Mom glared at him. "He did it on purpose."

"How do you know?" Dad shot back.

"I'm sorry," I said.

"I told you to leave the table," Mom insisted.

I started to get up.

"Sit right there," Dad said.

I froze.

Then Mom got up, banged her chair against the table, and went out on the back porch, letting the screen door slam behind her. Cleo came over and lay down at my feet, her head on her paws. Cleo always knows when there's trouble.

Nory excused himself and got up next. That left Dad and me. I felt like a prisoner. Dad wasn't eating, just staring out the window, his jaws locked together.

Finally I said, "I guess I'm finished, Dad."

He didn't answer.

I scooted my chair away and, when Dad still didn't say anything, went out front where Nory was waiting. We walked over to the high school. All the while we worked out in the weight room, I worried about what was going on at home. It was hard not talking about it. Once I did mention it to Nory, and he just said that some couples fight and some don't. Every time I looked through a magazine, at advertisements with a man and woman in them, I'd wonder if they were the kind of couple who got along or the kind who fought. But the people in magazines were always smiling. I decided to ask Nory again.

"What do you think's going to happen? With Mom and Dad?"

Nory went on working the bench press.

"I don't know," he said finally.

"Doesn't it get to you sometimes?"

"Not much we can do about it, is there?"

The thing about Nory is you have to sort of guess what he's feeling. He's not like me. Dad used to say it was as though somebody put a quarter in me and I couldn't shut up. He never said that about Nory. If you put a quarter in Nory, you'd get it back.

When we got home, whatever must have happened was over. We could hear the TV going in the den, and upstairs, Mom's bedroom door was closed. I sat on my bed looking through Nory's yearbook while he sorted through his school papers.

"Here's Mickey Johnson," I yelped, coming across a picture of a girl smiling real wide with her lips closed. (That's the way they do when they wear braces.) "She looks like she's got her mouth wired shut."

I showed the picture to Nory, and he laughed.

There was a tap on the door and Mom came in. Her eyes were red from crying, and she had a Kleenex wadded up in her hand. You know what's scary? When your mother cries.

At first she pretended she was fine.

"Well, how does it feel to be free for the summer?" she asked, sitting on the edge of Nory's bed.

"Great," said Nory, dropping another fistful of papers in the wastebasket. "Good-bye, history; good-bye, Spanish; good-bye, geometry I."

Mom smiled and turned to me, but her eyes were filling up again. "I'm sorry I overreacted at dinner. I was in a bad mood to begin with."

"I should have covered my mouth or something," I told her.

"That's not the point," she said, and pressed her lips together.

I sat slowly turning the pages of Nory's yearbook without really looking at them.

And then she started crying. She just put her head in her hands and sobbed, like a girl did once in social studies when she failed a test. I felt awful. All because of a belch!

"I'm sorry," Mom said as she wept. "I really didn't mean to do this, but I just can't take it any longer. I just can't."

My lips barely moved. "Take what?" I asked numbly.

"All this quarreling! This coldness!" Mom said, blowing her nose. "It just doesn't make sense to go on living this way."

My heart started beating time and a half. Nory paused, one hand over the wastebasket, then let another bunch of papers drop.

"I really think . . ." Mom said, ". . . I really

think it would be best for all of us . . . if Gene and I lived apart."

My muscles tensed; I felt as though my head was trying to pull loose from my shoulders.

Mom wiped her eyes. "Maybe I shouldn't be telling you all this, but tonight, after what happened at dinner, I knew that this quarreling had gone on long enough. I'm going to ask Gene to rent an apartment somewhere."

Something heavy seemed to be pushing down on me, pressing me flat against the floor. Nory didn't say anything, just went on shuffling papers.

"When are you going to tell Dad?" I asked finally. My voice was all squeaky.

"I don't know. Please don't say anything about it. I'll bring it up myself when I'm ready."

There was a time bomb ticking away in the Solomon household.

"This must be an awful shock for you," Mom said finally, "though I'm sure you've known that Gene and I haven't been getting along for several years. Is there anything you want to ask? To talk about? Nory?" She watched him anxiously, and when he didn't answer, she said, "Ted, you must have some questions. You're never this quiet."

Sure I had questions. I had lots of questions. *Do we go with Dad? Do we stay here? Where do we spend Hanukkah? Who will be around when I graduate? Who's going to tell Grandma Rose?*

But what I really said was: "We don't have to give up Cleo, do we?"

Mom stared at me. "Of course not. Why would you think that?"

I didn't know. It was the only question I could ask that wouldn't tear me apart.

"Well," she said finally, and her shoulders slumped. "Now you know. It's a relief, in a way, to get it out. But for now, this is just among the three of us. Okay?"

Nory waited until she went back downstairs. Then he dropped his whole notebook in the trash, looked at me, and said, "Happy new year."

I couldn't even answer. I lay back on my bed, staring up at the little spots on the ceiling where I bounced my superball. So this was what it was like, I was thinking. I'd always wondered about things like that: How does it feel to have cancer and find out your leg has to come off? How does it feel when your grandmother dies? You know what it's like when you find out your family is coming apart? It's as though nothing that ever happened to you before or will ever happen to you again could possibly be as important—that this is the only thing that matters.

Later, when the lights were out, I said, "It's all my fault, Nory. If I hadn't belched, maybe it would have blown over."

"If it hadn't been that, it would have been

something else," Nory said. "You, me, the dinner, the dog. . . . Anything can set them off." He stopped. When he spoke again, his nose sounded clogged. "I just wish they'd hurry and get it over with."

I kept swallowing, but I couldn't get rid of the lump in my throat. "No matter what happens, Nory, we're still family, you and me," I told him. "Deal?"

"Sure, Ted."

I was awake a long time. I knew Dad was sleeping on the couch in the den now because he keeps a pillow and blanket down there, and I wondered how he would feel when Mom asked him to move out. I didn't want to keep her secret. I wanted to open the window and yell it out for all the neighbors to hear. But I didn't. I finally went to sleep.

5

Uncle David and Aunt Sheila came over for Nory's birthday and parked their Cadillac in the driveway so no one would run into it on the street. Uncle David and Aunt Sheila are usually dressed as though they're going to a party because they usually are. When you work for a congressman, you go out almost every night.

Grandma Rose came down from Baltimore. Grandma is usually dressed as though she's going hiking, even when she's not. She always wears a pantsuit. She still gives me little treats when it's Nory's birthday and does the same for him. As soon as she presented Nory with his gift, she handed me a little dimestore compass.

"To take to camp," she said, "in case you should get lost."

At the table, I found three new pencils by my plate with my name printed on them, and when it came time for Nory to open his gifts, Grandma slipped me a roll of Lifesavers.

"Look at this!" Nory said, pushing the tissue paper aside. "A mask and snorkel! This is great, Grandma!" He didn't tell her that the lake at Camp Susquehannocks is muddy and that all you could see through a mask is your nose.

"For keeping an eye on the sharks," Grandma said.

Uncle David threw back his head and laughed. He's Dad's brother and looks the way Dad would look if he weighed fifty pounds more.

"When did you start worrying about sharks, Rose?"

"David, try to get smart," said Grandma. "You've heard of sharks in the ocean, maybe? Doesn't the Chesapeake connect to the ocean? Doesn't the Susquehanna connect to the Bay?"

Uncle David whooped again. "But the boys swim in a lake!"

"Oh," said Grandma. "Well, who knows what's in a lake? Water snakes, maybe."

"On to the next present." Aunt Sheila smiled. She and Uncle David had already given Nory a check, and they were in a hurry, because they had a reception to go to in Washington.

Nory picked up the next gift. Mom and Dad gave separate presents. Mom's was a Levi jacket and Dad's was a Walkman radio that Nory could wear when he mows the lawn. My gift to Nory was in a manilla envelope, inside a handkerchief box, which was inside a shirt box, which was inside a coat box, which was in the packing crate that brought our new vacuum cleaner. I used the Sunday comics for wrapping paper.

"Wise guy," said Nory, after he opened the coat box and found the shirt box. "You just wait till your birthday."

He kept opening boxes, and Uncle David kept looking at his watch. Finally Nory got down to the manilla envelope. Inside were a couple of *MAD* magazines.

"Hey, these are all right," Nory said, pleased.

Mom brought out a fudge cake with sixteen candles, only I had stuck on a trick candle that wouldn't blow out.

"Make a wish," Grandma said.

Nory thought for a minute, then took a big breath and blew. All the candles went out but one. He kept trying and trying, but it wouldn't go out. Aunt Sheila fidgeted around on her chair, and her bracelets clattered.

"Okay, Ted," Nory accused, turning to me, and I laughed.

But the custom in our house is that if you don't blow all the candles out, you have to tell what you wished.

"So what was your wish?" Mom smiled.

Nory hesitated. "Well, I wished that Grandma would still be here when I'm thirty—"

"Hear! Hear!" said Dad.

"I should live so long!" said Grandma, smiling.

". . . and that . . . we would all get along better."

Nobody moved. Uncle David and Aunt Sheila looked across the table at each other. I wondered if they knew about Mom and Dad.

Finally Mom said, "That's a noble thought, Nory—we should all get along better—people, nations, races. . . ." She went out in the kitchen for the ice cream.

"Tzu lange yoren," Grandma Rose said in yiddish.

"Yes," said Dad, lifting his glass and clinking it against the others. "To long life."

Uncle David got up and so did Aunt Sheila.

"Sorry we can't stay around for the cake, Nory, but we've got an energy bill pending in Congress and this reception's for the bigwigs. Got to go shake some hands."

“Thanks for the check,” said Nory.

“Be good,” said Aunt Sheila, pinching his cheek, which is about the dumbest thing you can do to a guy, if anybody wants to know. I was glad when they left. Nory and I got to eat their cake.

That evening Nory went off to the movies with some friends, and Dad asked me to help him hoe the garden. To tell the truth, I don’t get too excited about gardens. Every year Dad buys six tomato plants, a row of onions, a row of lettuce, and a couple of green pepper plants, and what have you got? A salad, that’s all.

He goes out every evening, though, and works when it’s cool. So there we were, side by side, all for the sake of some vegetables.

“They’re coming along nicely, aren’t they?” he said, examining a lettuce leaf. “We ought to be able to put this on a sandwich in another week or two.”

“When will the rest of the stuff be ready?” I asked, looking around.

“Well, we might get something in July, but August is the big month.” He pointed to the tomatoes. “See those over there? Those are Jetstars, and these are Supersonics. I’m going to see which produce the most. Every time we pick a tomato, we’ve got to mark it on a chart.”

Somewhere inside me there was a sadness that just kept growing and growing. Dad might not be here in August. He might not even be here in July.

The minute Nory and I left for camp, Mom would probably ask him to move out.

And suddenly there I was with the hoe in my hand, crying. I tried to keep the tears back, but they rolled down my cheeks, then onto my arms, making long white streaks in the grime. Dad had his back to me, gently tamping down the soft earth around the pepper plants, and I wondered what would happen if he wouldn't go? If he just told Mom no? Would *she* move out? Would they sell the house and send Nory and me to live with Uncle David?

When it got too dark to see, we quit, and I sat on the back porch with Grandma Rose, drinking lemonade with vanilla in it.

"Well, Ted," she was saying, "so you leave next Sunday for camp. Have you got a good sweater now, for when the nights are cold? Do you remember when your cousin Joseph almost got pneumonia?"

"You gave me a sweater for Hannukah," I reminded. Grandma gives me a sweater every year. I've got more sweaters than any kid in Kensington besides Nory, who gets them too.

"So I did," she said, remembering, and then settled back on the glider. "You're going to write to me, now? Every Friday a postcard, eh?"

"Okay," I told her. And then I said, "I want you to do something for me too, Grandma."

"Sure, sure," she said.

I didn't quite know how to say it. "I want you to keep an eye on things here at home and let me know what's happening."

Grandma Rose didn't look at me, just kept pushing her feet against the floor, and the glider moved back and forth. I could hear the faint *click, click* of her teeth.

"I don't make a very good spy," she said at last.

"You can call Mom now and then, can't you?" I suggested.

She looked over at me. "What's worrying you?"

"All sorts of things."

Grandma Rose sighed. "What will be will be. All sorts of things *could* happen, but most of them won't."

I really wanted to tell her Mom's secret, but I didn't dare. I stared out over the back yard, at the space in the darkness that was Dad's garden, and felt the lump rising in my throat once more.

"Well," Grandma said finally, "I will tell you everything I see with my own eyes or hear with my own ears, but a detective I'm not."

The thing about worries is that you get tired of them after a while. When Grandma Rose left the next day, all I could think of was how awful she was going to feel when she found out that Mom and

Dad were separating. But by Monday, when Dad took Nory for his driver's license, getting Nory through that test seemed the most important thing in the world. Because somewhere in the back of my head was the idea that if things ever got bad enough here at home, Nory and I could just jump in the car and take off.

Dad let Nory drive to the Motor Vehicle Administration, and I hung over the back seat, asking Nory questions from the driver's handbook:

"How many points for trying to elude a police officer?"

"Twelve," said Nory.

"If a pedestrian is in a crosswalk, you should—"

"Increase speed and run him down," Nory joked.

I turned some more pages. "What do you do if you die in a traffic accident and want to donate your kidneys and stuff to science?"

"Sign an organ donor's card in the presence of two witnesses," said Nory.

"Before or after the accident?" Dad quipped.

Nory carefully turned in the entrance of the testing area. There were policemen all over the place.

"Please don't hit anything," Dad murmured as Nory maneuvered between two squad cars and parked in the lot. Dad and I got out and stood around with Nory, looking over the driving course. It was as if we were seeing him off to war.

"Well," Dad said at last, slapping him on the shoulder. "Go to it, Nory."

"Have a good trip," I joked.

Nory was in the building for so long I began to worry they'd put him in jail or something. Maybe he'd missed so many questions they didn't think he ought to be out walking around. But he came out at last and got into Dad's Buick beside an officer carrying a clipboard.

"He must have passed the written test, Dad," I said hopefully.

"Keep your fingers crossed," said Dad.

I couldn't tell what was happening, but it looked as though they were just sitting there. Finally Nory got back out and felt around in his pockets.

"My god," breathed Dad. "He can't find the keys."

Nory found them at last in his shirt pocket and then got back inside. The Buick started up. The motor died. I closed my eyes.

"Now what?" said Dad.

Nory tried again. This time the engine roared and a cloud of smoke poured out the exhaust.

"Take it easy!" Dad pleaded.

The car crept forward, approaching a stop sign.

"Stop, Nory, stop!" I whispered.

The Buick stopped. Nory looked both ways. He signaled. The car made a left turn and started up the stretch in front of us toward the orange markers, where Nory would have to parallel park. Dad and I moved away so Nory wouldn't see us watching.

I wished I was out there with the broom boxes. I wished I could help guide him in with my hands. The Buick stopped, then began inching backwards.

"Cut it sharp, Nory," Dad said aloud. "Cut it sharp."

The back wheels hit the curb.

"Did he fail?" I asked Dad.

"He gets three minutes, and he can't touch a marker," Dad told me.

Nory pulled forward, then backed in again. Again the wheels struck the curb. I covered my face.

"His last chance," said Dad.

I could see Nory's shoulders rise and fall. For the third time the Buick lined up with the markers. Slowly it moved backwards. Slowly the wheels turned out, then in. Nory was parked.

"He did it!" I yelped.

We watched them go around the entire course.

The turn signals went on and off. Nory stopped and started on a hill. We watched him bring the Buick to the finish line. The officer got out and started around the car. Nory jumped out too, grinning widely, looking for us. When he caught Dad's eye, he held up the keys and waved to show us he had passed—and walked right into the policeman.

"My God," Dad said again.

I watched numbly as the officer set his cap back on his head. Nory was apologizing. The policeman was saying something too. Then they both went into the building.

Dad and I sat down on a wall and waited. All Nory's practice down the drain, I thought. Twenty dollars down the drain. Driver's ed down the drain. I hadn't worried about the right things. *Don't run a stop sign,* I'd told him. *Don't forget to signal. Don't hit a marker.* But I'd forgotten to say, *Don't walk into a policeman.*

And then the door opened and Nory came out. Smiling. He was a driver at last.

The only thing we had to do before Sunday was get our physicals. We do this every June. Mom drives us to the doctor's office over in the medical building and comes back an hour later to see what's what.

It takes a long time at the doctor's. First we have to sit in a waiting room with clowns and elephants on the walls. Mom says that when we get to be eighteen, we'll stop going to the pediatrician and see the family doctor instead. I don't know what's so special about eighteen—maybe your bones start growing different or something—but meanwhile we're stuck here with a roomful of picture books and blocks, while a lot of two-year-olds with runny noses push each other around. Nory and I usually pick out the worst bully of all and then, when his mother's not looking, make faces at him. He either starts crying, which is great, or makes faces back. Then his mother catches him and gives him a spank, which is even better.

The nurse finally calls us in to be weighed and measured, then gives us each a paper cup for a urine specimen and we take turns in the bathroom.

"Have some lemonade," I always say to Nory when I come out with my cup.

The nurse puts us in an examining room together and tells us to take off everything but our socks and undershorts. Once I had to go to the doctor just for a sore throat and the nurse still told me to take off my shoes. I asked Mom why, and she said it's so I won't hurt the doctor if I kick him. I'd never even thought of it till she told me.

"The doctor will be with you shortly," the nurse always says.

Shortly means about twenty minutes. The first thing we do is flip a coin to see who gets to go first and have it over with. We flip at the dentist's, too. Whoever wins sits up on the examining table and the other one sits in the doctor's swivel chair and looks at the picture of his wife and children. Sometimes a little kid will run up and down the hall opening all the doors and peeking inside. If any kid peeks in at us, we throw our shoes at him.

We usually each take a sucker from the candy jar if there are any lime or lemon, and then we look through the glass doors of the cupboard at all the needles and try to figure out what they're for.

"That one's for the eyeballs," Nory always says, pointing to a short one, "and the long one over there's for the belly button."

After we read all the certificates on the wall telling where the doctor went to school and study the pictures of how your arm's not supposed to look after a tuberculin test, we hear the doctor coming and dive back into our places.

"Well, well, the Solomon brothers," Dr. George always says when he comes in. "How's it going, fellas?" And the examination begins.

This time, though, after the nurse measured me, she put me in a room and I waited and waited but Nory never came.

"Where's my brother?" I asked, when the nurse stopped by to take my blood pressure.

"He's in another room." She smiled. "The doctor thought it best."

That really teed me off. Nory and I have always been together. After she left, I wondered if he could be in the room next to mine. Somebody coughed, and it sounded a little like Nory. I thought of the way we do sometimes before we go to sleep—one of us taps out the rhythm of a song on the wall and the other tries to guess what it is. I was thinking of tapping "America, the Beautiful," but then I wondered what would happen if it was Dr. George over there writing up a report. I was waiting for the cough to come again when the doctor walked in.

"I just saw your brother and he's fine," he said. "Now let's have a look at you."

"I thought I could be in the same room with Nory," I told him.

Doctor George got out his stethoscope and held it against my back. "Well, he's getting to the age when he needs a little privacy, you know. Take a deep breath, Ted. That's it. . . . Now another."

There are only two parts of the exam I don't like: when the nurse pricks my finger for a blood sample, and when the doctor examines my throat. As soon as he puts that stick on my tongue, I gag. I even gag when I watch him do it to Nory. That's why doctors wear white coats, so if you throw up all over them, they can change without going home for another suit.

"Well," he said finally, "I can't find a thing that should keep you from having a good time at camp this summer." He sat down at his desk and made a few notes in the chart. "Anything particular bothering you that I should know about?"

I wondered why he said that—if he could read trouble in my face.

"No," I lied. "Everything's fine."

He nodded. "School go okay this year?"

"Yeah. Everything's great."

"Well, then." He sort of slapped the edge of the desk and leaned forward. "You've got a healthy body there. Have a good summer."

When I had on everything but my shoes, I opened the door to get some air in the room. I could hear Mom down the hall a little way, talking with the doctor.

"I just wondered . . . there's been a lot of tension at home," she was saying. "You know, the end of school and everything. But they're okay?"

"Fine. They're both in good shape."

Nory came out of a room at the end of the hall—he hadn't been next to me—and we followed Mom to the car.

"What did you tell the doctor?" I asked him.

"What do you mean?"

"How come he put you in a room all by yourself? What did you talk about?"

Nory shrugged. "Nothing."

"Did you ask him about hair on your legs?"

"Oh, knock off about that," Nory said irritably. "Just drop it, will you?" But when we reached the car, he said, "I'll drive, Mom. Let Ted sit up front with me." And then I knew he wasn't mad.

We spent the rest of the day packing. Mom brought us heaps of fresh laundry—lots of tee shirts and shorts and sweat socks. One pair of dress slacks apiece and two short-sleeved sport shirts to wear at the Saturday night socials, where people actually dance with each other. I slipped in a jar of Mum in case I should start to stink at camp. I even took along Charlie. You never know when you might need a tapeworm.

Even though we've been going to camp every summer for the last eight years, Mom still gets teary-eyed when we leave. She says it never really seems like summer until we're home from camp and lazing around under the lawn sprinkler. I think she means it, too. I never felt that my folks didn't love us; they piled all the love they couldn't give each other onto Nory and me.

Dad drove us to the bus. It's an old yellow school bus with "Camp Susquehannocks" painted on the side, and it starts down in Roanoke, comes up through Richmond, then stops at Washington, D.C., before heading over the Pennsylvania line. There's another bus that comes down from New York, and another from Ohio. They all manage to get to camp on the same day. All the girls hug each other, the boys yell, and the decibel level goes up to ninety. The first hour at Camp Susquehannocks, all we do is talk.

On the way to the bus, though, Nory and I were pretty quiet. I sat in the back seat with one arm around Cleo, wondering what it would be like for her alone in the house with Mom and Dad. It was Dad who did the talking.

"Well, Nory, do you think you'll still remember how to drive when you get back?" he joked.

Nory smiled. "Won't take long to get in practice."

The trees and buildings moved silently by outside the car window. I could see Dad watching me in the rearview mirror.

"You probably won't recognize the garden when you get home, Ted. Vines should be full of tomatoes. I'm betting on the Jetstars. How about you?"

"I don't know," I said. I really didn't care about those tomatoes. I felt like a traitor. Nory and I knew what was going to happen after we left, and Dad was just thinking about his garden. I wondered if I could give him a hint, a warning. Finally, without looking at Nory, I said, "If . . . if anything happens, Dad, while we're at camp. . . ."

"Listen," Dad said, "if anything happens up there, any trouble at all, you just call and I'll be there in a minute to pick you up. Don't you worry."

I leaned back against the seat and stared out the window. Nory didn't say a word. We passed a billboard with a man and woman on it. The man was smearing suntan lotion on the woman's shoulders. They were smiling. I wondered if Dad ever put suntan lotion on Mom.

I was worried about Dad, but about Nory, too. He never lets his feelings out, never lets go.

"You always seem to have a great time at camp," Dad continued, "but I don't ever want you to feel that we're sending you away, that we're making you go."

We pulled into the parking lot, and I saw the yellow bus. Nory was getting our bags together, and there wasn't time to say anymore to Dad. I really don't know what I would have said if there had been.

I got out of the car.

"Stay," I said to Cleo when she started to follow. Then I reached in through the window and petted her. If Grandma wrote that my folks were fighting, I'd ask her to take Cleo.

The way you wake up at Camp Susquehannocks is somebody stepping on your cot. I could tell by the weight of the foot that it wasn't my brother.

"Up! Up! Up!" a voice demanded, and the weight lifted from off my cot and bounced over to Nory's. By the time I got one eye open, Brian Shumsky had sprinted along the entire row of beds and disappeared into the back room to shower. On the other side of the bunkhouse, Mitch Horlick switched on his tape recorder.

"Some boogie music to wake you guys up," he said.

I rolled over and wondered if I could get by

wearing yesterday's socks. Probably not. Bunk counselors were particular about things like that. Mitch and "Shum," as we called Brian, were both starting college in the fall. Just last year they were waiters like Nory.

Mitch is dark—hair, eyes—even the hair on his arms and legs. "Gorilla," we call him. Shum is just the opposite. Blond. A Greek god, and his skin is tanned the color of wet sand. Girls fall all over both of them, but especially Shum.

Nory got up and pulled on the white terry cloth shorts he'd been saving for camp.

"Hey! Check out Nory's shorts!" someone yelled.

Mitch whistled. "You're looking studly in those shorts, Nory," he said.

Nory was pleased.

Our bunkhouse is called the Weasels. I could have been in the Nighthawks or the Rapids, but I wanted to be with Nory. I sort of had this plan about camp, see. I wanted us to learn to do as much as we could for ourselves—wanted to see if we could get along without parents—so that no matter what happened, Nory and I would make it okay.

I headed for the "cubby," as we call our locker room, to get my towel. Bernie, the pudgie guy who sleeps across from me, was trying to sneak his jeans on over yesterday's shorts, but Mitch caught him and threw his Levis up on the rafters where they stayed until Bernie took his shower.

As we went out the door for line-up, Shum said to me, "Ted, when we get back, you make my bed and straighten my locker." I beamed all the way to the dining hall. My very first morning as a Weasel, and *I* had been chosen.

Line-up, though, is something else. The first thing it is is dumb, because there's a roll call. As though, if somebody was missing, we wouldn't know already. And then the head girls' counselor and the head boys' counselor tell us all the marvelous, exciting things they have planned for the day, while we sort of lean on each other and hold our eyelids open with our fingers.

By the time we reached the dining hall, though, we were awake. The kids from each bunkhouse eat at their own table, and all the counselors were asked to stand up and introduce themselves. When Mitch and Shum stood up, the Weasels yelled and slapped the table, and Bernie made embarrassing noises by holding his arm up to his mouth and blowing.

"Someone's too big for his britches," Mitch said when he sat down. "*Someone's* going to get cornflakes in his cot tonight."

Nory looked real good as a waiter. He wore a big white dish towel around his waist and went from table to table holding a tray of toast high in the air with one hand. He learned to do it last summer, but this year he was even better at it. I figured it must have something to do with driver's ed.

The waiters eat last, but they always get the best and the most of everything. Nory and I have a system. If there's something I really like, I signal as he goes by my chair.

Sausage, I mouthed as he passed our table.

"Later," he whispered, and dumped three extra packets of jelly by my plate.

The main thing about camp is it's loud. It's loud when we arrive. It's loud when we leave. It's loud whenever there's a race or contest of any kind. But mostly it's loud in the dining hall.

Every so often Mitch would say, "More noise! More noise!" and we banged our spoons or pounded our feet. The Willows, a bunk of teenage girls sitting two tables away, suddenly started a chant:

"Debbie Gould, wants it bad.
Brian Shumsky. Go, Brian, go!"

Last year I didn't understand some of the chants, but this year they made sense. It's just one of those things you appreciate when you get to be thirteen, I guess.

If two people are named in a chant, they're supposed to stand up and kiss in front of the whole dining hall, but they never do. Debbie Gould hid her face on the shoulder of the girl next to her, laughing. Shum, though, stood up grinning, with his arms wide open, and Debbie half slid under the table.

Mitch got the Weasels singing. He knows all the commercials on TV and the songs from all the shows, and he made us sing the theme song from *Gilligan's Island* before he let us have more scrambled eggs.

And then, while I was taking a bite of toast, while Bernie was drinking cocoa, while Nory was refilling the water glasses, while Joe Reiling, smallest guy in Weasels, was spooning cornflakes, Shum yelled, "Freeze!"

It's my favorite word at camp, even better than "studly."

No matter what you're doing when a counselor yells "Freeze," you stop. In the middle of chewing, of slicing, of pouring, of swallowing. You become one big hunk of marble, because the first guy at the table who even breathes, practically, has to scrape and stack the plates afterwards.

Everyone at the other tables stood up to watch and laugh and try to get us to move.

"Hey, Ted!" someone yelled. "There's a bug on your toast!"

But I just sat there with the bread halfway in my mouth, my teeth in the crust.

The problem was that Nory was right in the middle of pouring water and he didn't dare tip his hand backwards. The water kept coming and the glass overflowed and the puddle spread across the table and trickled down on Joe's jeans. He squirmed, and it was Joe Reiling on garbage detail for that meal.

I hung around the door waiting for Nory afterwards.

"Sausage," he said when he came out, and slipped me an extra piece in a paper napkin.

As we passed the post office, the clerk called us in.

"Got a package for you guys," he said.

We were mortified. *Nobody* gets mail the first day of camp. The first *week,* hardly.

"From R. Rose, Baltimore," the nosy clerk said, tilting his head back and looking through the bottom half of his glasses.

"My grandmother," Nory told him, taking the package.

We were going to hide it outside the bunkhouse till we could smuggle it in, because Grandma usually sends chocolate chip cookies. No one was inside, however, so we sat on Nory's cot and ripped off the paper.

"I don't believe it!" Nory said, when he lifted the lid. "Sweaters!"

"Button-down-the-front sweaters!" I added disgustedly.

We couldn't let the Weasels see us in those. We couldn't even let the Weasels know we got them, so Nory climbed up and hid the sweaters in the rafters. Then we opened Grandma's letter.

Dear Ted and Nory,

I want you should have new sweaters. You've grown since Hannukah, and it's possible the old ones don't fit. I got them at Penney's, and a better bargain you won't find.

I hope you are having the time of your lives and keeping busy. You should worry about anything, worry about catching your death of cold. I know what temperature it gets in Pennsylvania. I hear it on the news. You want to make your grandmother happy? Wear your sweaters.

Love and Kisses,
Grandma Rose

P.S. There are M & M's in the pockets.
P.S. again: Everything goes fine at your house.

Nory had to climb back up again to get the M & M's. But I was thinking about that letter. It was written before we'd even left home. Grandma certainly wasn't much help.

And suddenly I felt really angry—angry at Grandma, because she didn't realize how bad things were between my folks; angry at Mom for wanting Dad to move out; angry at Dad for not making her happy. I wished that Nory and I could stay at camp always and never go home. But if Nory was bothered, he never let on. He's so cool sometimes it scares me.

I was still mad the next day. Each thud of water against the underside of the raft felt like a punch in the back. Each puff of cloud overhead looked like a fist. I was partly mad because I'd wanted to talk with Nory about it some more that morning but couldn't find him. Now that we were in the same cabin together, he was always off with somebody else.

"Damn!" I said aloud. Sid, a big guy lying beside me, stirred, but didn't turn his head, and I went on staring at the sky, my hands knotted stiffly over my stomach.

What if Nory and I got some mysterious disease and went into a coma? What if we went out in a canoe some morning and never came back? What if we were walking along the highway and got hit by a truck? It would serve my parents right. I imagined them bending over our hospital beds, begging us to open our eyes; I saw them huddled together on the bank as firemen dragged the lake for our bodies; I pictured them with their arms around each other at our funeral, saying, "Why couldn't we have gotten along better when they were alive?"

Angry tears collected in the corners of my eyes. If Mom and Dad needed a calamity to get them back together, maybe Nory and I could think of something.

Then I remembered that Sid broke his collarbone at camp two years ago while his folks were back in Connecticut getting a divorce, and the collarbone didn't change a thing. And that John Jennings and his folks went on a big trip to Alaska together, and the day after they got back, his parents split up. Alaska didn't change a thing, either.

At the other end of the raft, Bernie and Joe Reiling were horsing around. I felt the spray from the splash as Bernie fell off, and then the tipping sensation as he climbed back on again.

"Cut it out," I said crossly. "Can't you guys just lie still?"

"What's eating Solomon?" asked Joe.

"Let him be," said Sid, and the others settled down. But Sid turned toward me. "What's wrong?"

I shaded my eyes with one arm. Mom had said that the secret was just between her and Nory and me, but I didn't care. The guys at camp didn't count.

"My folks are splitting up," I said.

"Oh," said Sid. "That's really rough."

I rolled over on my stomach and watched two girls in a canoe paddle by. They each wore green and white tee shirts with "Camp Susquehannocks" printed on the front and their breasts came to points just above the "q" and the second "n." I wondered if I was the only jerk who noticed things like that.

It was a relief to tell Sid about Mom and Dad, even though he couldn't help. It was as though someone had opened the top of my head and let some of the anger out. This was where I belonged, not back home listening to them quarrel.

Nory and I used to talk about starting a camp ourselves someday. We told Grandma about it, and she said we could call it "Solomon's Glory." I don't know—I think it should sound sort of Indian, like "Solomon's Susquehannocks." Or maybe we should just leave out the Solomon altogether and call it Keeyumah or something.

The girls were paddling around the raft and coming back on the other side. Sid lifted his head and watched them. Sid has pimples on his back. They weren't there last summer. Every year something changes; no one's quite like he used to be. I guess that was bothering me, too.

There was a softball game that afternoon. Every Tuesday the boys play and the girls watch; on Fridays the girls play and the boys watch. All boys above twelve are organized into teams, the greens and the whites. There are some sports you get to choose at camp and some you have to play, and baseball was required. You can't get out of playing in the weekly game unless you're in a wheelchair or something. Nory and I were greens.

I picked up my glove and trudged out to the baseball diamond behind Mel Kramer, boys' head counselor, and the rest of the guys. If there's anyone I want to be like when I'm thirty-five, I guess, it's Mel. His build is thick and square, and when you see him across the clearing, he looks like a television set on legs. Every time he breathes, practically, his biceps go up and down. He's got hair all over, even in his ears.

I like everything about him—the way he talks, the way he laughs, the way he smells, even—a sort of metallic, perspiration smell, a lot different from Uncle David.

So there I was, following along behind Mel. Every place he stepped, I stepped, careful not to catch the back of his heel. Boy, he had big feet.

Somehow the baseball diamond looked a little smaller than I'd remembered. Maybe the trees were closing in, I decided. You just turn your back, it seems, and something changes.

Mitch was captain of the greens, and Shum took over the whites. Naturally, most of the girls, sitting on the grass, began rooting for the whites, just because Shum looks so studly.

We were up to bat first. I don't know which I hate more, being a batter or being first baseman. Mel always arranges these games so that we change positions after every inning. By the time summer's over, every boy will have had a turn at almost everything. Mel even keeps track on a chart. He says if we're going to goof up, we might as well do it here, surrounded by friends. I hoped that all those workouts in the high school weight room would help me hit the ball further than third base. The whites' pitcher wasn't very good, though. He didn't get a single ball over home plate, and I ended up walking to first.

In the second inning, Sid was pitcher for the whites, and I felt the familiar rock in the pit of my stomach. Sid pitched really fast. The first batter struck out. Then Nory struck out. The girls were going wild. Debbie Gould, her yellow hair falling around her shoulders, was jumping up and down, screaming Shumsky's name. I don't know why he didn't just go over, kiss her, and put her out of her misery.

And then I had the bat in my hands, all the

girls were looking at me, and Sid was leaning back, winding up for the pitch.

The ball streaked past me and landed in the catcher's mitt.

"Strike one," yelled Mel.

Sid made a crazy face at me out on the pitcher's mound. Then he wound up again and let fly. The bat merely tipped the ball.

"Strike two," yelled Mel.

"Put your hands closer together," Nory said from somewhere behind me.

I adjusted my grip and kept my eyes on Sid. The ball came again, and I swung.

Smack. I hit the ball with all my strength. I looked for it out around third base and then I saw it high in the air over left field. It was sure a pretty sight. I couldn't take my eyes off it.

"*Run,* Ted!" Nory yelped.

I was only halfway to first when someone caught the ball, but I didn't care. It was the farthest I'd ever hit it.

Then it was me out in left field and all the big guys on Shumsky's team were up to bat. Joe Reiling, though, was pitcher.

The balls came right over home plate, just where they were supposed to be, but so slow and easy you could have run along beside them.

Whup. The first batter hit a grounder that

rolled right past the second baseman, and he got to first.

The balls kept coming, and pretty soon the bases were loaded. And then I saw Sid coming up to bat.

Nory, who was playing center, moved over a little in my direction, in case I needed help. We always get on the same team if we can and keep an eye out for each other.

Sid hit the ball on the first crack. It made an arch over third base and then it was coming down behind me. Nory was too far forward to help. I put both hands up in the air and started running backwards, my eye on that ball, hoping I wouldn't trip.

"What'cha doing, Solomon? Praying?" someone jeered.

Whop. The ball landed in my glove and rolled off the edge. My legs buckled and I went down on my knees, but I got it again before it could touch the ground and held it against my chest.

"Out!" yelled Mel Kramer. "Good going, Ted! Real good!" I tried not to smile too wide.

And then, when I was coming in off the field and passed the girls, someone said, "Good catch, Ted."

I looked around. It was one of the bunk counselors from the Willows, Marilyn Davis. She had large hazel eyes and kept her dark hair tied in a pony tail. She was seventeen. And she was smiling.

"Thanks," I said, and went behind the backstop.

I didn't know she knew my name. I wasn't even sure she'd ever noticed me. I pretended to be concentrating on the guy at bat, but I was really watching Marilyn—the way her tan legs crossed at the ankles, the way she held up her ponytail to cool the back of her neck. She saw me looking at her and smiled again.

I had this awful temptation to sniff under my arms to be sure I didn't stink. I promised myself I wouldn't look at Marilyn again, and then—I'd be looking. And suddenly I was thinking about the dining hall and how nice it would be if the Willows ever made up a chant about Marilyn and me.

"Marilyn Davis, wants it bad.
Ted Solomon. Go, Ted, go!"

I wondered what I would do if that ever happened to me. I imagined Marilyn blushing and hiding her face behind her hands. I imagined me, standing up like Shum did, holding out my arms to Marilyn and laughing. Somehow, it didn't work. The first time I tried it, Mitch would yell, "Freeze!" and I'd be stuck like that for a whole minute.

Saturday night was my first social at Camp Susquehannocks. Only the thirteen to sixteen-year-olds and their counselors can go. Suddenly I wished I was twelve again.

"Hey, Nory, how do you dance slow?" I asked that morning. We were alone in the bunkhouse, and I figured I could learn before the Weasels came back from the lake.

"I thought you knew," Nory said. He was shining his loafers with an old tee shirt. "You were doing okay at your bar mitzvah."

"Those were only cousins," I told him. "Come on. I've got to know by tonight."

Nory put on Shum's Diana Ross tape. "You've

just got to move in time with the music, that's all, and not bump into anybody. Put one hand here"—he placed my hand on his back—"and hold your other hand out like this."

I swallowed.

"Now," he said. "Wait for the beat. You got it? Okay, start moving."

I promptly stepped on his foot.

"Why didn't you move backwards?" I asked.

"I didn't know which way you were going," Nory said. "You've got to give me a sign. You have to move your whole body forward, not just a foot. Push against my hand or something so I'll know."

I tried again. This time we moved together, but when I went sideways, I forgot to bring my other foot along, and Nory stumbled over it.

"This is stupid!" I said disgustedly.

"You'll get it," Nory encouraged.

We tried again. By the end of the first song, I had backed Nory into the cubby and bumped into a door, but at least we got through it.

There was a round of applause from the window. The Weasels had been watching.

"Such a bea-utiful couple!" Sid gushed.

"Oh, bug off," said Nory, and went back to shining his shoes.

Maybe it was just nervousness or maybe it was thinking about boys and girls together that got me worrying about Mom and Dad. But suddenly, around four o'clock that afternoon, I had a terrible feeling that something had happened to them—that maybe Mom had asked Dad to move out and there had been a big fight.

I got a quarter out of my cubby and walked out to the pay phone along the highway. I told the operator I was calling collect, and then I heard our phone ring. My heart started to pound. I'd never called home before from camp, and I wondered which parent would answer. Mom would say, "Ted! What's the *matter?*" Or Dad would say, "What's up? Anything wrong?" I didn't quite know what I'd tell them.

What happened was that nobody answered. The operator let it ring about twelve times and finally I hung up. Then I remembered that Mom usually shops on Saturday afternoons, and sometimes Dad plays tennis. I felt pretty silly. It's a good thing they didn't answer. Now I could stop worrying about what was happening to them and concentrate on what was about to happen to me.

We began getting ready for the social as soon as dinner was over. There was so much steam coming from the showers that Mitch had to turn on a fan to keep the mirror from clouding over. Four blow dryers were going at once, and Shum went around fixing collars, telling each guy how studly he looked, even when he didn't. I was all dressed before I remembered the Mum and had to stick a hand up each sleeve to smear some on my armpits.

Adam, a new guy at camp this year, was combing his hair down over his forehead to hide his acne.

"Hey, Adam," Sid called from the other end of the bunkhouse. "Gonna try a little Frenching tonight?"

"What?" said Adam.

All the guys guffawed.

"You know . . . tongue kissing," Joe Reiling told him.

Adam blushed. "Oh," he said. And then, "Why not?"

Bernie swaggered through the room smelling of English Leather cologne. He had on a pink sport shirt and gray slacks with a crease as sharp as folded paper. *"I'm* going for second base," he said with a smirk.

"Ha!" Sid said. "You haven't even got up to bat yet."

On the way to the field house, Nory turned to me and pulled his lips back. "I got anything stuck between my teeth?"

"No, you're okay," I said.

"Smell my breath."

"Oh, jeez, Nory!" I said.

"Please," he whispered. "I've got to be sure it's not garlicky or anything."

I let him breathe in my face.

"It's all right," I said. "Sort of like celery." I could tell that he was nervous, too. Maybe we could just sneak off together—go crawl up on the roof of the dining hall and forget the dumb social. But I knew we'd never get away with it. One of the rules is that you don't sneak off.

If you break a rule at camp, it's Mel Kramer who calls you on it. The rules are: no drinking, smoking, fights, drugs, or sex. No food in the bunkhouse, either. But Mel's got a motto: "I'll let you beat me short as long as you don't try to beat me long." He knows we all keep cans of soda in the toilet tanks and that we get food from home on visiting day. He knows that the older guys kiss the girls and lie about doing a lot more. But if you pull a big one on Mel, it'll be your last summer at Camp Susquehannocks. With a counselor who breaks the rules, it's worse. He's out, just like that. Gone the same day. *Good-bye, counselor. Write when you get home.*

All the guys got to the field house before the girls did.

"Smell that!" Nory said to me. "The Nighthawks must have used up a whole bottle of cologne."

Mel Kramer was disc jockey for the evening. He was wearing a blue blazer and I figured that the women counselors must all be mad about him. He had just put on the first record when the girls came in.

I don't know what I expected. I knew they wouldn't be in long gowns or anything, but I suddenly discovered I didn't know what to say to a girl in a sundress with her whole back showing. It seemed as though half the girls were in sundresses with their backs showing. When I danced, for Pete's sake, where was I supposed to put my hand? I looked desperately around at the other guys. Everybody was smiling. I never saw so many teeth in my life.

"*Ev*-erybody!" Mel Kramer was saying over the microphone. "I don't care whether you have partners or not. Everybody out on the floor for the first number."

That was easy. The music was fast and no one was touching anyway. When the song was over, I tried sneaking off to one side, but all the bleachers had been turned around backwards so we couldn't sit down. I looked at my watch. An hour and twenty minutes yet to go.

The next number was fast, and so was the next. I'd sort of smile at a girl and face her as I danced, so even if she was someone else's partner, no one knew the difference.

And then the lights dimmed, the tempo changed, and suddenly bodies were moving closer together, while others, mine in particular, were scurrying over to the side to get out of the way.

I leaned against the bleachers and watched. Shum and Debbie Gould were dancing about as close as pages in a book. All over the floor couples were swaying slowly in time to the music. How did people get paired up so quick? I wondered. Maybe these were leftover romances from last summer.

Joe Reiling edged up beside me.

"I just realized we can't get out," he said, motioning toward the doors. Adult counselors were stationed at every one of them. Obviously, nobody was leaving the field house, especially in pairs.

One of the counselors from The Echoes, a girls' bunkhouse, came over and asked Joe to dance. That's one of the rules at camp too, Nory told me, that bunk counselors have to dance every third dance with a camper, not another counselor. This is so no one gets left out.

Joe turned to me like he was going to be sick or something, but the counselor grabbed his hand.

"Come on," she said. "I don't bite."

Joe moved out onto the floor like a zombie in a body cast.

I looked at some girls standing across the room and wondered if I should ask them to dance. There were all kinds of reasons why I didn't. One had on high heels that made her a lot taller than me. Another was wearing a fussy blouse with a ruffle in back, and I wouldn't know whether to put my hand above or below it. One was laughing. You don't ever ask a girl to dance if she's laughing. I was trying to think up a reason why I couldn't dance with the fourth girl when Mel switched to a fast record and the lights came on again.

"How you doin'?" Mitch asked me, walking by. His hairy arms were covered by a tan dress shirt, rolled up to the elbows. "You want me to line up somebody for the next slow number?"

"No," I told him. "I'm doing okay."

"You better get out there, Solomon," he said. "I'm going to be looking for you."

I managed a grin. "Sure," I said.

I reconnoitered the gym to see if there were any doors left unguarded. A window, even. When the next slow number began, I decided to look for Nory. If ever I needed him, it was now. Maybe, if we were standing off to one side talking, no one would hassle us. I made my way around the dancing couples, avoiding Mitch, pretending I was on my way somewhere, that I had some place to go. There were even counselors standing by the restrooms making sure that kids didn't hide out in there. But Nory would think of something. He knew the fieldhouse inside and out. This was our big moment to do something really wild—make a grand escape. Now that we were in the same cabin, this was our year to become a legend—the year of the Solomon Brothers.

And then I saw him, with his hands on a girl's waist. She had both her arms around his shoulders and they were sort of moving back and forth in time to the music, looking into each other's faces and talking. I turned away.

"How about me, Ted?" said someone, and I practically walked right into Marilyn Davis's chest.

Sure, I said, except that only my lips said it. Absolutely no sound came out.

"Sure," I said again, and this time I sounded like Donald Duck.

If Marilyn noticed, she didn't let on. She slipped one hand in mine and put the other on my shoulder. For a moment my mind went blank. I couldn't remember a thing Nory taught me, and then I felt Marilyn's body move to the left so I moved too, and finally, there we were, dancing.

She had on a red dress, but it had a back to it so there wasn't any question about where I should put my hand.

"It's a pretty night," Marilyn was saying. "Everything's out but the mosquitoes. I didn't get a single bite on the way over."

"Yeah," I said. "Me too. I mean, I didn't get any either. Any bites."

I wished I could start that all over again, but Marilyn didn't seem to mind.

"I even saw a bat flying around the trees near our bunk. Have you ever seen one up close?" she asked.

"Huh-uh," I said. "I mean, yes."

"They look like mice, don't they? There was one in my locker last year. I kept the door open so it could run out, and when it spread its wings and flew, I thought it was leaping at me!" She laughed, and I laughed with her.

Things were easier now. I only bumped into somebody else once. Marilyn smelled like some kind of flower. Tulips, I guess. I was trying to figure out how tall I'd be next year. If my forehead came up to her chin right now, by next year I'd reach her nose, and the year after that . . . .

"Are you coming back next year?" I asked her.

"I hope so. My folks are after me to get a real job, though, so I can help with college tuition."

"Yeah, I know," I said.

She looked down at me. "How about you? Are you coming back?"

"Forever, if I can."

We laughed again. I liked the way her eyes creased at the corners.

"Forever's a long time," she said.

And then the number was over, and I didn't want it to be. I knew that slow dancing would never be so scary again because of her, and somehow I wanted to thank her. Thank her for not wearing a backless sundress, even.

"Thank you," I said.

"I enjoyed it," Marilyn told me, and she just barely squeezed my hand. I mean, hardly anyone else would have noticed if they'd been me, but I could tell. It was just a soft press of her thumb and forefinger against my palm, and then she turned and walked toward a group of friends.

There was a lot of talk in the bunkhouse that night after the social was over.

"How'd it go, Ted?" Nory asked me.

"Great," I told him.

"You get to second base, Bernie?" Joe Reiling asked.

"Yep."

"Bull!" said Sid. "He couldn't even find them."

Shum got some cans of Pepsi out of the toilet tank and I saw him shake one of them up real hard back in the cubby. He handed that one to Bernie. When Bernie opened it, it fizzed all over him.

"Hey, Bernie! Even your can's full of hot air!" Mitch said, and we laughed. I was really feeling great and studied myself in the mirror. Not bad. Maybe I wouldn't grow up to look like Woody Allen after all.

When I was hanging up my shirt, I found a couple letters that had come that afternoon. Nory had picked up the mail and forgotten to tell me. One was from John Jennings and the other from my dad. I opened John's first.

Hi, Ted!

How's it going? I called your house last week to see if you could go swimming, and they gave me your address. Sure is nice not having to get up in the morning for school.

There's a stamp convention in Washington this month and there will be a special booth where you can trade stamps. I'm going to take some of my duplicates and see what I can get.

In August, I'll be staying with my dad in Rockville, and we're planning to go white water rafting this fall. He said I could bring a friend, and I thought maybe you'd like to go. I'll call when you get home. Watch out for snakes.

John Jennings

In a P.S. he told me he just had his thirteenth birthday, and he added thirteen exclamation marks after it.

There was something about his letter that made me uncomfortable. I didn't want to hear about guys going off to visit their fathers—didn't want to hear about fathers living by themselves in Rockville. I wadded up John's letter and chucked it under my cot. Then I opened Dad's.

Dear Ted,

I'm wondering where you are reading this: Under a tree? In the dining hall? On your cot? I hope it's under a tree and that the sun is shining and there's a breeze, because that's what I think of when I remember camp. I suppose I've forgotten the bugs and the blisters. Anyway, I hope you're having a good time.

You should see the tomato plants! Every day there are more yellow blossoms. Something's been getting at the lettuce, though, and I think it's a rabbit. I wouldn't mind sharing it with him if he'd just nibble on one plant instead of taking a bite of each of them.

I'm getting ready to sand and varnish the floor in your bedroom. It's a good time to do it while you guys are gone, so watch it when you come back, or you'll slide right out the window. Haven't heard from either of you since you left, so I guess things are going well. I'm not sure who will be coming up on visiting day, but you can count on someone.

Lots of love,
Dad

I lay back on my bed, staring up at the rafters, listening to the Weasels kid around. The happiness evaporated and I felt as flat as a piece of cardboard. Mom hadn't told him yet. We would have to go on waiting.

"Who was that girl you were dancing with last night?" I asked Nory.

Our paddles dipped in the water together as the canoe moved under a willow branch and shot out again on the other side.

"Which one?" said Nory.

I paused, my paddle above the surface, and the canoe turned slightly. "There was more than one?"

"I wouldn't dance all evening with the same girl," Nory told me.

I frowned at the back of his tee shirt and fell in with his rhythm again.

"You looked like you'd known her all your

life—the girl in the pink blouse," I said. "You sure weren't looking out for me."

"Why should I?" said Nory. "It seemed like you were doing okay for yourself."

We were passing Camp Morning Lark on the opposite side of the lake, where all the cabins were built to look like teepees. It only accepted girl members, and their fathers had to be millionaires or something. Then we rounded the bend and I concentrated on Nory again. I guess I felt better knowing that he had a lot of girl friends, and that the one in the pink blouse wasn't special.

"I got a letter from Dad yesterday," I told him, changing the subject.

"So did I. All he said was that he's getting the car tuned so it will be in good shape when I get back."

"Mom hasn't told him," I said.

"Probably not."

"You know, Nory, we ought to get prepared."

"What do you mean?"

"Well, anything could happen. There could be a fight. They could go to court. We've got to start thinking about what we're going to do if the judge asks us who we want to live with—Mom or Dad. I couldn't choose, could you?"

Nory shook his head.

"Well, then, we'd just have to go off and live by ourselves somewhere."

"Yeah?" Nory said. "Where? In a cave?"

"There are places," I told him, "but we have to start thinking about it now. We ought to be learning how to catch our own fish and make our own baskets and stuff."

Nory turned around in the canoe and stared at me. "You're serious!"

"Of course I'm serious! The trouble with you, Nory, is you never think ahead."

"Mom says she's asking Dad to move out, and already you've got us living in a cave, eating out of baskets?"

"Okay, Nory, okay. You just go on dancing with the girl in the pink blouse and I'll learn all the stuff myself. You're going to need me someday."

I just couldn't believe about Nory. All the years we were in separate cabins, Nory would say, "Wait till you get to my bunkhouse, Ted. We're really going to have a great time." Well, it wasn't working. Everytime I had an idea for something to do, something really original—like a big escape from the field house the night of the dance—Nory had other plans. Now when we needed to do some serious planning, Nory took it as a joke.

When we got back to the dock, I went to the activity room to sign up ahead for the second half of camp. We have to have four hours of planned activities a day, and two of those have to be classes. I saw that Nory had signed up for music appreciation, bird study, orienteering, and photography. I put my name down for fishing, archery, basket-weaving, and leatherwork. He might be able to get us to a wilderness somewhere to hide out, but what would he do after we got there? It would be me who caught our food and made our dishes and everything.

That evening I wrote a postcard to Grandma: *I can't believe that everything's fine at home. You said you'd let me know. Have you called Mom lately? How's Cleo? Ted.*

I didn't tell her a thing about camp. I wanted her to know how it feels to get a letter without any information in it. I especially didn't mention the sweaters.

The Fourth of July is a big deal at Susquehannocks. Everyone's supposed to help decorate his bunkhouse, and the camp store sells rolls of crepe paper streamers and stuff. The trick is to be original and win first prize.

"We could paint flags on all the windows," Bernie said.

"Nah, the Nighthawks did that two years ago," Mitch told him.

"What about painting our bodies?" said Sid. "You know, stars on the cheeks, stripes on the forehead. . . ."

Shum shook his head. "Someone does that

every year. Don't you remember the time the Willows all painted stars on their kneecaps and did a tapdance?"

We slouched down on our cots.

"I've *got* it!" I yelped suddenly. "Red, white, and blue streamers looped from rafter to rafter."

The guys stared.

"What's so original about *that?*" asked Sid.

I went back in the cubby and came out with something in my hands.

"A blue crepe paper streamer," I said, "a red crepe paper streamer, and a white tapeworm named Charlie." I held out the jar.

Actually, Charlie was more yellow than white, but he'd pass.

The guys whistled in appreciation, and Nory and I stretched it out so they could see how long it was. More murmurs of approval. Even Mitch and Shum were impressed.

"You're a darn good Weasel," Shum told me.

That was my glory day.

The decorating wasn't quite as easy as it looked because Charlie came apart in two places and had to be stapled. But when all the campers came through to see each other's bunkhouses, Charlie was the chief attraction.

"Gross!" Debbie Gould shrieked when she saw it.

But Marilyn Davis wasn't afraid to touch it.

"Where did you get it, Ted?" she asked, and I told her about finding it in the science room wastebasket.

She walked over to one end to see if Charlie had any eyes. "You know what I'm thinking of being, Ted? I haven't really told anyone yet. A veterinarian. Does that seem strange to you?"

"I think you'd make a wonderful veterinarian," I said.

She smiled at me, her eyes creasing at the corners again, and I smiled back. I think I went on smiling all day. All night, practically. Thirteen was definitely turning out to be one of the best years of my life. Not counting the trouble with Mom and Dad. Or Nory.

That evening we all sat on the bank by the lake and watched the water pageant. Canoes with lighted lanterns moved slowly in patterns on the surface of the dark water, and some of the older girls, with flashlights attached to their swim caps, formed pinwheels and sparklers. For all I knew, some other guy was sitting beside Marilyn Davis, there in the dark, with his arm around her, but I didn't care. I was one of the first people she had ever told about wanting to be a veterinarian, and I went over it again and again in my head. For a moment I panicked, thinking I might have said, *You'd make a wonderful vegetarian,* instead of *veterinarian,* and I wondered if that's why she smiled at me, but then I was sure I said it right.

When the pageant was over, we all sang our camp song:

> *"White as the sky above,*
> *Green as the rolling hills,*
> *Colors that we all love,*
> *Susquehannocks.*
> *We roam it night and day,*
> *We'll leave it when we must,*
> *And yet our hearts will stay*
> *In Susquehannocks."*

One by one the lanterns went out on the canoes, and finally the lake was dark. Walking back to the bunkhouse beside Nory, the smell of pine around us, I felt that no matter what happened at home, I could take it, as long as I could keep coming here every summer. I wondered if Nory felt the same way about camp. About me. I wasn't sure anymore.

The next day was even better. Shum yelled "Freeze," and while we locked ourselves in position, Mitch went around the table jazzing things up. He put a cup of iced tea on Bernie's head, so that if the guy *did* move he'd have it all over him. He put one of Sid's hands in the beef stew.

I sat in delicious anticipation as Mitch came around to me, hoping that he would do something to make everyone in the dining hall sit up and notice.

"Hey, Ted, look what I've got for you!" Mitch said. And while the kids at the other tables shrieked with laughter, Mitch stuck a french fry up each of my nostrils.

Adam broke the freeze by laughing, and then Shum was slapping me on the back saying, "Good show!" Man, I felt great. One freeze with french fries up the nose was worth five doubles with the bases loaded in an intercamp game.

I got a letter from Mom later that week. Nory got one too. It was short and said exactly the same thing she wrote to Nory except she turned the paragraphs around.

Dear Ted,

I guess no news is good news, and that you and Nory must be having a marvelous time—otherwise we would have heard. I do miss you both—the house is far too quiet when you're away, and Cleo mopes about looking like a lost soul. But I'm glad we could afford to send you to camp this year and hope we can continue to do it, because I know how much it means to each of you.

I suppose this is bound to be an upsetting summer for us all. However things turn out, though, I want both you and Nory to know that we love you very much. You're great guys to have around. You'll always have the same people to love—you'll just have us in different combinations, that's all.

Much love,
Mom

It was beginning to get to me. There were times I felt I didn't care what happened as long as it happened fast. I found myself reading Mom's letter again and again, worrying about every word. What did she mean about "different combinations"? I even wondered if maybe she was planning to run off with Uncle David and Dad with Aunt Sheila or something. I mean, once you let the worries in, they play volleyball in your head.

I got the panicky feeling that maybe there was something more I could do to keep them together—that I still hadn't tried hard enough. It was awful not knowing what was going on back there. And then I remembered that once, on Grandma's birthday, one of my aunts sent her a bouquet of flowers from Chicago. I couldn't figure out how you could send flowers all the way from Chicago, but Dad said you could do it by phone. I wondered what would happen if I sent a dozen roses to Mom along with a card saying, "I love you. Gene."

I remembered that dumb birthday card I'd sent Mom once, signing Dad's name, but somehow this seemed different. Even if she discovered it was from me instead of Dad, maybe it would make her realize how much I wanted them to stay together. I didn't have much time. Any minute she could be asking Dad to move out.

Before I could lose my nerve, I walked up to the camp office and asked to use the phone book. In the back, in the yellow pages, I looked up "flowers." I found "florists" instead. One advertisement said, "Flowers by wire. Just pick up the phone and say charge it."

I took a deep breath, picked up the phone, and dialed the number.

"Simpson's Flowers," a woman said.

"I'd like to send a dozen roses to Kensington, Maryland," I told her.

"Certainly. What color would you like?"

"What?" I said. I didn't know they came in anything but red.

"We have white, pink, yellow, red. . . ."

"Red." I gave her Mom's name and address and told her what I wanted her to write on the card. She said she would call a florist in Kensington and arrange for delivery.

"Credit card?" the woman said.

I knew then there was a hitch. Nothing could be this easy. Mom had almost received a dozen red roses, and now she wouldn't.

"I . . . I thought you could just charge them to my father," I said.

"Do you have his credit card number?" the woman asked. "I have to have a number."

"I guess I don't," I told her, and hung up.

I sat in the woods a long time that afternoon thinking about all the things I'd tried that never worked. Even if I had sent the roses, they probably wouldn't have helped. It was a relief in a way to think that there wasn't anything I could do. But in another way it was like giving up on Mom and Dad, and that's about the emptiest feeling in the world.

Visiting Day is always the third Sunday after camp begins, halfway through the program. To tell the truth, most of the older kids are glad when it's over so they can get to the tennis tournament on Sunday night in the field house. It's the younger kids who get excited when their folks drive up.

I really didn't think much about it Sunday morning. When one o'clock came, however, and there was no sign of either Mom or Dad, I felt a little uneasy. Usually they were here early and were among the last ones to leave. But as I stood on a hill overlooking the parking lot, I couldn't see a sign of Dad's Buick. I wondered if things were worse at home than I had imagined. When one-thirty came and they still weren't there, I was sure something had happened. I thought about those news stories where parents shoot each other and all the neighbors claim they had no idea, the couple seemed so nice and friendly. I imagined Uncle David driving up and saying, "Ted, I'm afraid we've got bad news. . . ." Then I realized they were probably arguing so hard that the time just slipped by. I was mad all over again that I'd bothered to worry.

"No show, Ted?" Mel Kramer said, coming up behind me.

I thrust my hands in my pockets. "Oh, I suppose they'll be along pretty soon. One of them, anyway."

Mel stopped and stood with me there in the pine trees.

"They know this is Visiting Day?"

"They know," I said, and somehow the bitterness in my voice leaked out.

Mel studied me for a moment, then looked at his watch. "I'm going out to the highway to meet the two o'clock bus. Want to come along?"

"They wouldn't be on the bus," I said.

"I know, but I could use the company."

I was glad to have something to do. Nory was in the dining hall serving cake and punch to all the parents, and I was feeling sort of left out. I got in step with Mel, stretching my legs to keep up with him. Every year a few of the parents come by bus, and it's Mel's job to be out on the highway to meet them.

He looked down at me a time or two, and I realized that I was scowling. I was angrier than I'd thought. Angry at waiting for them to show up. Angry at waiting for the other shoe to drop. For Mom to tell Dad; for Dad to get mad; for one of them to move out.

"You sure you want them to come?" Mel asked me finally.

"No," I said honestly. "No, I'm *not* sure."

Mel slowed down a little. "Problems?" he asked.

"My folks are splitting up," I told him.

Mel reached up and pulled a pine cone off a branch, juggling it from one hand to the other as he walked. "You just find out?"

"Mom told us before we came. She said she was going to ask Dad to move out, but she hasn't. And I'm getting tired of the whole mess."

"You'd like to have it over with," Mel said.

"You know it!" I picked up a pine cone myself and heaved it as hard as I could against the trunk of a tree. It made a hollow *thunk* sound, and a piece flew off. I threw another.

"Everyone's upset," I said. "Nory, Grandma, the dog, even. . . ." I turned to Mel suddenly. "Are you married or divorced?"

Mel stopped juggling the pine cone and tossed it lightly over to one side. “I *was* married,” he said, “but Sara died. An accident.”

I sucked in my breath. “Lord, I’m sorry,” I said. I was, too.

“Yep, we’d just bought a farm near Frederick, got a couple horses—we were going to raise beef cattle and live off the land—ride out everyday on horseback and see how things were going. Big plans. And one snowy morning she was driving the pickup into town for feed and went off the road. Just like that—all the plans. . . .”

I stared straight ahead, afraid to look at Mel, knowing that this was a private moment.

“But you know something, Ted? No matter what happens to people—to families—nobody can take away the good times you’ve already had. They’re yours to keep.”

I kept walking, keeping pace with Mel, kicking little clouds of dust out behind me in the dirt. But finally I told him, “I hardly remember the good times.”

“That’s because it hurts. But you will.”

We had reached the bus stop at the end of the long drive and stood leaning against the beech tree that marked the entrance.

“I don’t know what I’d do if I couldn’t come here,” I said. “Right now I feel it’s the only home I’ve got. The only thing I can *count* on, I mean.”

He nodded. "I feel that way sometimes. Nobody back at the farm but a hired man. After I've been away awhile, though, I begin to miss the place, even without Sara."

Far down the highway, I could make out the silvery outline of the bus. Mel and I moved out from under the tree and watched as it came closer. When it slowed down, a few men and women stood up, reaching for boxes and bags on the shelf above them.

"Come down to the lake tomorrow and help me work on my canoe," Mel said.

"Okay," I told him. Mel had been carving a dugout canoe for the past two summers, and this was the year he said he would finish it. It was sort of a special honor when Mel Kramer invited someone to work on the canoe. You got to carve your initials in the side.

The door of the bus opened and people began getting out. I started up the lane toward the camp again.

"Ted!"

I turned, and there she was, coming down the steps one at a time: Grandma Rose.

11

"Here," said Grandma. "Help carry."

"I didn't know you were coming," I said, going back and taking two packages from her. One of them rattled like chocolate chip cookies, and the other thudded softly like brownies.

"I didn't know myself until yesterday," she said. "Elaine called last night and we decided that I should come this year. I've never been here, you know." She laughed when she saw me sniff the packages. "Now don't go getting fat."

We walked back up the lane cushioned with pine needles. Grandma Rose had on her earth shoes, which curled up in front, and I took shorter steps so she could keep up with me.

"What's happening at home?" I asked.

"That we'll talk about later," she said. "Where's Nory?"

"In the dining room. We're serving cake and punch."

"Well, I shouldn't," said Grandma, "but if I'm going to go hiking like this, I need my nourishment."

"Sure." I smiled.

A table at the front of the dining hall had been covered with a white cloth and green streamers. Parents were standing around holding cups of punch. I found a chair for Grandma and brought her four little squares of cake, each with a different color of frosting.

"I'll just eat one," she told me, but nibbled them all.

"Grandma!" Nory said, startled.

"Surprise!" she cried, and hugged him.

"Where are Mom and Dad?"

"Not coming this year. Things piling up at home." Grandma wiped her lips. " '*I've* never seen that camp,' I told Elaine. 'Why don't you let *me* go?' So here I am."

"Well . . . great! Let's show you around," Nory said.

While he found a place to hide our packages, I introduced Grandma to some of the guys. It's funny, but they didn't sound like the same people when they talked to Grandma. They didn't even look the same. Bernie, for instance, stood with his hands behind him and sort of rocked back and forth on his heels. Grandma thought the guys were wonderful.

"So polite!" she said as we took her outdoors.

We went on a tour of the meadow, the baseball diamond, and the field house, and ended up by the lake.

"Such a lot of space!" Grandma kept saying, her pocketbook swinging on one arm of her lavender pantsuit. "I should have had such a camp when I was your age!"

She didn't care for the lake, though. Too deep, she said. Too dark. If someone fell in, you'd never see him again.

"You know what my mother used to give me when I went swimming at Coney Island?" she said. "A red cork to wear around my neck. If I ever lost my footing and was floating just under the surface, she said, the cork would bob about and someone would notice." Grandma was quiet for a moment. "If I sent two corks. . . ."

"No way," said Nory. "No corks."

"Every little bit helps," Grandma retorted.

We realized when we were out on the wharf that all the other campers and their parents had gone back up to the dining hall. Angry dark clouds swirled overhead, and a crack of thunder came so suddenly that Grandma grabbed hold of my sleeve. We made it as far as the bandstand before the rain came pelting down.

"Well," said Grandma, breathless from the excitement, "it can't last forever. We'll wait it out." She pulled the edges of her jacket close together in front and looked at Nory and me. "Where are your sweaters?"

Nory gave me a quick glance. "Back at the bunkhouse."

Grandma shook her head. "You'll catch pneumonia out here in the damp."

"Listen," I said, "what's happening at home?"

Grandma Rose hugged herself a little tighter and squinted out across the water. "It's not good, that's what."

I tried to make it easier for her.

"Mom and Dad are separating, aren't they?" I said.

Grandma sighed again and pressed her lips together. For a moment I saw tears in her eyes. "That's what Elaine said yesterday. She's told Gene to move out." Her voice trembled.

"When?" Nory asked. "When did she tell him?"

"Yesterday morning."

I tried to think what I was doing yesterday morning. Cleaning out the cubby; making my bed; having another helping of French toast. . . . I wondered if that's when she told him—at breakfast—the two of them sitting there with Cleo looking on. Mom would reach for the butter and say, "Gene, I want you to move out." Is that the way it had been?

"What did you say, Grandma, when she told you?" I asked finally.

"I should say something wise, maybe, like Solomon?" Grandma said. "What's to say? 'Elaine, you should think about this, maybe.' That's what I said, and she told me she'd been thinking about it for the last three years. 'Three years isn't so long,' I said. 'Marriage is a lifetime.' And she said that's what was the matter—it seemed like a lifetime already."

Grandma Rose shrank down in the collar of her lavender jacket, leaning forward on the bench so the rain couldn't reach her. We could see campers and their parents standing in the doorway of the dining hall. The paint on the "Welcome" sign had started to run. Mel Kramer was going from parent to parent shaking hands. The camp director was there, and even the owners. I wished I was back up there with the Weasels, but they seemed a long way off. Now that I had got Grandma talking, I suddenly wanted her to stop.

"Except for my brother Sam, there hasn't been a divorce in my family that I know of," she was saying, shaking her head. "Your great uncle Theodore and his wife never got a divorce, even though they went their last seven years without speaking. 'Elaine,' I said, 'What about the boys?' And she said it was worse on you if they stayed together." She looked at Nory. "Is that true?"

Nory just shrugged and stared down at his hands.

" 'Are you going to have two houses?' I said to Elaine. 'You going to have two cars? You think you've got troubles now, you should try living apart.' But she just said, 'It's worth it, Mother.' Now what kind of an answer is that?"

I was looking at the lake, at the way the sun shone halfway across the water and then stopped. The storm cloud was only over us. It was crazy.

"Well," I said to Grandma. "At least she's told him."

Grandma Rose didn't answer. We all sat quietly as the rain slacked off. The sky was beginning to brighten on our side, a cold white light, and the air was cooler. Rain dripped off the eaves around the bandstand. Down on the lake, the wind ruffled the surface. Parents were beginning to move around outside the dining hall.

Grandma stood up. "Let's go back to the bunkhouse and get your sweaters," she said.

"It's not cold," Nory protested. "I'm fine."

"You think I don't know cold?" Grandma asked, and pointed to the goosebumps on Nory.

We trudged on ahead of her, trying to decide what to do.

"Keep her outside while I crawl up and get them," Nory whispered.

But when we got to the bunkhouse, Grandma barged right in.

It couldn't have been worse. All the Weasels were there except Shum and Adam, all sitting around on their cots eating the stuff their parents had brought. Nory introduced Grandma Rose to the guys she hadn't met and tried to get her outside again, but she said, "The sweaters, Nory."

Nory's face turned as pink as Sid's sport shirt. Without a word, he got on a chair and swung himself up to a rafter. Hand over foot, he crawled along from beam to beam, until he reached the corner, Grandma and the Weasels watching speechless from below. Then he reached into a dark corner, took out a dusty box, and tossed it down to me. The lid came off. Out tumbled two orlon, button-down-the-front Penney's sweaters, the tags still dangling from the sleeves.

The Weasels stared. Grandma stared. And finally she said, "You really *did* hate those sweaters, didn't you?"

We walked her back up the lane at five. The sweaters were crammed in a net shopping bag that Grandma Rose keeps folded up in her purse at all times. She said she could still get a refund, seeing as how they were never worn.

"You know, Nory," she said, "we've got to be honest with each other. It won't do to hide how we feel—you and Ted and I. You don't like sweaters that button down the front? I'll get you another kind."

"Grandma," said Nory, "we don't like sweaters at all."

Grandma shrugged. "So I'll exchange them for jackets, maybe. For flashlights, even. You need flashlights?"

Nory stared straight ahead. "All I need is Mom and Dad to stay together."

Once in a great while, a feeling slips out in spite of himself. Even Nory can't hold them all in.

Grandma sighed. "That's something I can't get for you, Nory. I would if I could, but I can't."

We stood in the shelter on the other side of the highway with some of the parents and promised to do a better job of writing each other. The bus came, and Grandma climbed on.

"How's Cleo?" I yelled after her, but the door of the bus swung shut, and whatever Grandma said, I didn't hear.

The first three weeks at camp we lose all track of time because there are more weeks ahead than behind us. But after Visiting Day, everyone goes bonkers. We know that whatever we wanted to do at camp that year—whether it's make a bull's-eye or kiss a girl or row around the lake—we'd better hurry and get done, because everything ends on August 1.

Even the tricks the bunk counselors pulled on us got wilder. Bernie had been eating on Shum's cot and left crumbs all over the sheets. Shum grabbed him, wrestled him down, and wrapped him in fly paper. There wasn't one of us Weasels who didn't wish it was him. Bernie claimed he couldn't get out of the stuff and walked around camp like that for an hour.

Classes for the second half of camp had begun, and I turned out to be pretty good in archery. The first morning the counselors taught us to string the bows. Then they gave us each ten arrows and got out of the way. I'd never shot an arrow before, but by the end of class, I'd managed to hit the target eleven times and practically got a bull's-eye.

"Nory," I said later, "you ought to sign up for archery."

"What for?"

"In case."

"In case of what?"

"We ever need to shoot a rabbit or something."

"Shoot a *rabbit!*" Nory said. "Why would we want to do that?"

I shrugged. "You know. To eat. I mean, if we had to."

Nory just laughed.

"I *mean* it." I frowned. "What if Mom and Dad get a divorce and can't agree who gets us and the judge sends us to live with Uncle David and Aunt Sheila? What would you do then?"

"Go live with Uncle David and Aunt Sheila, I guess," Nory said.

"You want to put on a tie and go to a party every night and shake hands with a bunch of congressmen?" I bellowed.

"I'll worry about it when the time comes," Nory said.

That really made me mad. Nory doesn't even try to look out for himself, and whatever happened to him would happen to me, too.

"Mud-face!" I yelled. Nory doesn't like for me to call him names, and I hardly ever do, but this time I was really angry. "You're just going to take whatever comes! You let people walk on you. You're a mud-face, Nory!"

"Oh, shut up," Nory said, and walked away.

My mouth felt dry, like there was dust in it. The Solomon System wasn't working the way it used to. We were finally in the same cabin, Nory and I, but we were growing further and further apart. I stood looking after Nory as he disappeared over the hill, and then I wheeled around and headed for the lake. Mel was there working on his dugout canoe, and I remembered his invitation.

"I'm here," I said dully, as though he couldn't see for himself.

"Good," said Mel.

I watched for a while. "Looks like it's almost done," I told him.

"Another week, maybe." Mel had been working on the canoe a long time—slowly, he said, to give the exposed wood time to season. He picked up an adz—a sort of curved ax—and showed me how to hack away at the sides, the wood chips falling into the bottom of the boat. I was afraid I'd chop a hole in it, but the adz followed the shape of the canoe, and I did okay.

"Where'd you learn to make one of these, anyway?" I said, feeling more sociable.

"Had a Seminole friend once," Mel said. "He'd watched his great-grandfather make a dugout and remembered."

I worked on the inside, and Mel worked on the stern.

"I enjoyed meeting your grandmother," he said.

"Yeah. My parents didn't make Visiting Day, so she came." I paused, then told him: "Mom's asked Dad to move out. It's finally happened."

"Oh."

"Maybe he won't even be there when we get home," I said, and felt my anger rising again. "Wouldn't that be something? Start out for camp with two parents and find only one when you get back—like the other had been vaporized or something?"

"Hey! Easy! Easy!" Mel said, grabbing hold of my arm, and I realized I was hitting the adz hard against the side of the canoe. "One good thing about you, Ted—you let your feelings out."

I examined the canoe and was glad I hadn't

done any real damage. I rubbed it with my hand. "Nory's the one who holds back," I said. "He acts real cool, but some day he'll just erupt, I'll bet."

"Talking's pretty important," Mel said. "Some people say it doesn't really solve anything, but it sure lets out some of the steam."

I had a blister on my hand after the first fifteen minutes, but I kept working. You have to work a whole hour on the canoe before you can carve your initials on the bow.

T.E.S. I carved at last. Theodore Everett Solomon. As long as there was a Camp Susquehannocks, as long as the canoe was around, people would know that T.E.S. had been there.

By lunchtime, I was more sad than mad about Nory, so I waited for him afterwards. I just sort of fell in step beside him, and as we passed the post office, we saw a blue envelope in Nory's slot. It didn't look like Mom's stationary or even Grandma's. There was an M.J. in the left-hand corner.

"Who's M. J.?" I asked Nory, and then I came to a stop. "Mickey *Johnson?* Is *that* who it's from?"

"Probably," said Nory, and stuck the letter in his pocket.

"*She's* writing you here at camp?" I said in amazement.

"I suppose so," said Nory.

I just couldn't get over it. I couldn't figure out

what they had to say to each other. But Nory had clammed up again, so I didn't ask anymore about that. I was quiet for a while, and then I asked what I was really thinking.

"Hey, Nory, we're still a team, aren't we—you and me?"

He kept on walking. "Why wouldn't we be?" he answered.

I didn't feel a bit better.

What I was waiting for—what the whole camp was waiting for—was the carnival. It's an annual thing at Susquehannocks, put on for the campers by the counselors. The profits go to a home for retarded children. For a whole week no one's allowed in the field house, and then the carnival opens with games and prizes and contests and booths where you can buy all kinds of junk your parents will probably throw out when you get home. Last year we even had a kissing booth, but I didn't go in it.

The carnival is one of the camp events where all ages mix. For the first hour, in fact, every camper over ten is assigned a camper under ten, and we're supposed to go around the field house helping this little kid have a good time. After the hour's up, we can have the carnival to ourselves. It's supposed to make us feel like one big happy family. What it always makes me feel is glad I don't have any little brothers or sisters.

This year I was assigned a five-year-old boy named Jake, from the Muskrat bunk. This was his first year at Camp Susquehannocks, and he was absolutely bug-eyed. I'd noticed him before in the dining hall the day Mitch stuck french fries up my nose. He came over to stare at me—never laughed, just stared. Some little kids are like that—real serious.

He was wearing a King Kong tee shirt and basketball shoes that looked like they were a couple sizes too big. On our way over to the field house, this kid says to me, "When do we hunt for the eggs?"

"What eggs?" I said.

"The eggs the bunny brings."

"That's Easter, Jake," I told him.

"When do we eat the turkey, then?" he wanted to know.

"That's Thanksgiving," I explained.

And when we walked in the gym and Jake saw all the balloons and streamers, he asked, "When do we get the ice cream and cake?"

"That's birthdays, Jake," I said.

I wondered how his mother stood him. No wonder she bundled him off to camp.

And then I had this thought that maybe, somewhere back in Ohio, his parents were getting a divorce. Maybe his dad was marrying a woman who celebrated Easter and he was spending holidays with his mom who kept Passover and in the summer they sent him up here for the Fourth of July.

Not only couldn't he build a shelter or cook a fish or shoot a rabbit, but Jake didn't even know his holidays. I suddenly felt very sorry for him, like maybe I was the only friend he had in the world.

Jake and I really lived it up for the next hour. I taught him skee-ball, helped him with the ring toss, and bought him nine chances to hit a lever that would dunk Mel Kramer in a tub of water. Jake made it on the ninth try, and Mel gave a blood-curdling yell as he went in. Jake loved it.

We ate cotton candy, and I took him to the bathroom twice and finally got his fortune told in the gypsy's tent. ("A tall dark-haired woman will shortly enter your life," she said. I asked Jake later what color hair his mom had, and he said brown.) There was time for just one more game of skee-ball, and then I had to return him to the Muskrat's bunkhouse.

With the smaller campers out of the way, though, the tempo really picked up. I was on my way over to the magic show when I saw Marilyn Davis sitting in a booth marked "Honeymoon Suite." I stopped.

She had on a yellow dress and was laughing with Mitch. I took a step closer. There was another sign inside the booth, on a door to a back room. It read:

For five tokens, I'll show you something you have never seen before and will never see again.

I stood there as though my shoes had been nailed to the floor. I couldn't imagine what Marilyn was showing people in that back room. When Mitch walked away, though, I walked away, too. I went around the whole field house before I got up the nerve to go back. Then I stood behind a popcorn machine and watched while guys paid five tokens to go in the back room with Marilyn, one at a time. I checked my watch. A minute later, they each came out. Smiling.

I cornered Sid after his turn.

"What happened?" I asked.

"Wouldn't you like to know?" He laughed.

I couldn't stand it any longer and went to Marilyn.

"Hello," she said.

"Hi." I couldn't think of anything else to say.

"You want to lose five tokens?" she asked playfully.

I managed a little laugh. "Sure. Why not?"

She opened the gate of her booth, and I followed her into the back room, a broom closet, actually. It was Marilyn who shut the door.

There was an old velvet love seat in the room and a lamp with a shade that had little glass triangles around the bottom.

Marilyn sat on the love seat, and I sat down beside her. It was very warm in the closet.

"Okay," said Marilyn. "I promised to show you something you've never seen before and will never see again. And you have to promise that you won't tell anyone else what it is."

I nodded. I could feel a bead of sweat run down behind one ear.

Marilyn reached into the pocket of her dress and pulled out a peanut. She broke open the shell and took out a kernel.

"No one has ever seen this little peanut before," she said, holding it in the palm of her hand, "and no one will ever see it again." Then she popped it in her mouth and swallowed it.

To tell the truth, I was relieved. I started to laugh. Marilyn laughed, too.

"And now," said Marilyn, "so you won't feel cheated. . . ."

She leaned forward and kissed me. Right on the lips. Right there beneath my nose. I didn't even shut my eyes. I think I went cross-eyed.

When I came out, I walked right into Nory and hardly even noticed. I didn't care how many other guys were in line. A minute with Marilyn Davis was worth more than a freeze with french fries up the nose. Worth more than being covered with fly paper, even.

It happened the fifth week of camp. There was a letter in Nory's mail slot that afternoon from Dad, addressed to both of us, and we knew right away what it meant. We had to get to a basketball game, though, and needed to read that letter in private.

"Tonight," Nory said, and stuck it in his jeans.

After waiting so long for something to happen, I was angry that it had—angry that the letter came just before our big game. No matter when it came, though, it was never a good time. I didn't want Dad to move out. Didn't want Mom to leave, either. I wanted them both. And I was mad at them both.

I was going to be playing on a basketball team for the first time, not just fooling around. The captains got to choose their own teams, and Nory had been made a captain. He promised to pick me.

I was amazed at how much lower the basket seemed this year. Last summer, and all the other summers, the backboard seemed up near the roof, but this time I made a basket right off, and everyone in the bleachers cheered.

During the half, Mitch threw a lot of balls so we could all practice shooting, and I went pounding down the floor and whammed mine hard against the backboard.

That's for Mom, I said to myself. I retrieved the ball and aimed again. Bam! *That's for Dad.* The heck with Kensington, I thought. I didn't need them. I didn't need anybody.

We lost 47 to 44, but it was close enough to feel we had done okay. I figured that after the game, Nory and I would go off somewhere and read that letter, but he was talking with a bunch of girls.

It figures, I said to myself. I didn't need Nory, either.

I went swimming, and then it was time for dinner.

"Hang around afterwards," Nory said as he passed the Weasels' table.

I sat waiting for him on a bench outside. Everyone else had gone down to the lake.

"Coming to the canoe races, Ted?" Mel Kramer asked, going by.

"I'm waiting for Nory," I told him, and he went on.

I could see the dock from where I was sitting. There was going to be a color war. Half the canoes had green flags on them, half had white. I leaned back against the building and thought about Dad's letter. Maybe he had an apartment by now and was writing to give us his new address and phone number. *Call me anytime.* Maybe that's what he'd say.

Nory was the last waiter to come out. He had to stay and help scrub the stove, and the races had already started when he sat down on the bench. He opened the letter and read it aloud.

Dear Nory and Ted,
This is a hard letter to write, but I don't imagine it comes as a complete surprise, as Grandma Rose must have talked to you about it when she was there. As you know, things have not been going well for the last several years between Elaine and me, and I guess we both knew that we were heading for a showdown after you boys left for camp.

We've come to the mutual conclusion that it would be better for all of us if we were living apart. Neither of us likes the bickering that has been going on, and it's been hard on you too.

The question now is which one of us should move out. Elaine has the idea that it should be me, but I don't quite see it that way. In any case, things are sort of at a stalemate. Maybe when you boys get back, we can all sit down and discuss it. You might have some ideas on the subject yourselves.

I love you.
Dad

Nory didn't read that last line. I had to read it myself. In fact, I couldn't even get the paper out of Nory's hands, he was gripping it so hard. And suddenly he stood up, crumpled the letter, and started down the hill toward the lake.

"Nory?" I said. "What's wrong?"

"You know what they're trying to do, don't you?" he muttered. "They're going to dump the decision on us. *We* decide who goes and who stays. To hell with that!"

He was walking so fast I could hardly keep up. I stared at him. I'd never seen Nory like this before.

He didn't take the path toward the dock, though. He walked the other way, toward the boat house.

"Where you going, Nory?" I asked, catching up with him.

"Getting away for a while, that's what." He fairly spit out the words, and when he saw that all the canoes were gone, he said, "Where are the blasted canoes?"

"At the races," I told him.

"Where are the damn *rowboats?*" he yelled.

I looked down toward the races. The judges were sitting out in the lake in the rowboats.

Nory swore again and headed up the path, where the weeds grew tall and the ground was more sandy. He stopped and kicked a tree. Hard. Then kicked again. He was acting like a crazy man, and it scared me. Then, about fifty yards down, we came to the dugout canoe.

He stopped, and I thought he was going to step over it there in the path. He paused for a minute, then suddenly bent over and began pushing it into the water.

"Nory, no!" I said. "No! Don't! Mel hasn't even had it out yet."

"Shut up," said Nory.

"Where are you *going?*"

"Just out, that's all."

"You don't even have a paddle."

"So what?"

The dugout was heavy and made a groove in the dirt as it moved toward the water. Then it glided on. Nory steadied it.

"You coming?" he asked.

"We can't!" I protested. Nobody was allowed to take a canoe out without signing the log. And never without life jackets.

Nory shrugged and started to get in himself, and I had a sudden vision of him going out in the middle of the lake and drowning. Or going over to Camp Morning Lark and tearing down their dock or something—anything to get the anger out.

"Wait," I said, and grabbed the bow, climbing over and slipping in place.

The dugout moved forward a little, then settled down in the sand.

"Push off," said Nory.

I turned around, putting my arms down into the dark water and pushed hard against the bank. The canoe moved out.

Nory and I sat in the bottom. There weren't any seats. We rode low in the water, so low that we could put our arms over the side and paddle with our hands. The canoe traveled slowly and jerkily along the bank, away from the races at the other end of the lake. We rounded the bend, and then we were out of sight completely.

The sun had already set behind the teepees of Morning Lark, leaving streaks of crimson across the sky. The teepees loomed up black against it, their crazy topknots of poles like tassels on peaked hats.

"Stupid teepees," Nory said, his teeth clenched. He quit paddling suddenly and turned around facing me. His hands gripped the sides of the canoe, and he looked as tense as a cat ready to spring. His body just didn't seem to bend in the right places.

I sat there frightened, silent. It looked as though any minute he might just turn the canoe over and us in it.

"You know what?" Nory said finally. "Until today, I just shut them out. Just closed them off—Dad and Mom both. It's like there's a little door in my brain, and every time they start in at each other, every time there's trouble, that little door snaps shut and I don't let them get to me. But now Dad's put his foot in the door and I can't get it closed." His voice broke. "I can't get the damned door closed."

He was crying without making a sound. I was scared.

Please don't, Nory, I started to say, and then I realized it was exactly what he needed. I couldn't remember the last time Nory had cried. The last time he let me *see* him cry, I mean. Still, I didn't like sitting out there in the lake with Nory crying, without a paddle even.

I don't know how long we were there, because neither of us was wearing a watch. The sky had turned to purple and the trees on both sides were only clumps of gray. We'd drifted a long way from the bank and were just floating around in circles.

"We'd better get back, Nory," I said after a while, but if he heard me, he didn't let on. He just kept talking and talking, as though I was hardly there. About how the folks seemed to get along okay when he was five, and they seemed to get along when he was ten, but now that he was sixteen and had all kinds of worries—like going to college and getting drafted—the family was falling apart.

"Maybe they didn't get along as well all these years as we think, Nory," I suggested.

"Do you remember that amusement park in Virginia?" Nory said. "I was nine and you were six and we all got Mom to go on the roller coaster with us?"

I nodded.

"You remember how scared she was, and how she sat in the car behind us with Dad, and he had his arm around her—the way she was holding onto him? Didn't it look to you as though they'd stay together forever?"

I couldn't remember, to tell the truth. All I remembered was holding onto Nory.

"Listen, Ted, no matter how hard they try to push the decision on us—who goes and who stays—we're not going to make it for them."

"Sure, Nory," I said.

I was thinking about what he'd said about all his worries. I had worries, too. If Dad moved out, who would teach us to change a tire? To shave? To do the income tax?

Something was moving over the water toward us. As it got closer, I could make out a man in a rowboat, and finally, as he drew up, I recognized Mel. I swallowed.

Nory didn't see him at first. He had slumped down again, his head resting against the edge of the canoe. But when Mel got alongside, Nory jerked his head up, startled.

"Well," Mel said at last. "At least it floats."

I stared at my feet. I didn't know what to say.

Mel moved down to the end seat in the rowboat, reached out, and took hold of the dugout.

"I'm so mad at you guys I can't see straight," he said. "You've broken about every rule in the book tonight, and what I feel like doing is whomping the daylights out of you. What the *hell* made you do something like this?"

I started to tell him, then decided to let Nory do it.

"I just wanted to split for a while," Nory said. "I would have taken one of the other canoes, but they were all in the races."

"You didn't even know if the dugout was stable, Nory." Mel was yelling now. "You took your brother with you—no life jackets—no names on the log. . . ."

"I know," said Nory.

Mel studied him in the half-darkness. Nory's face was still streaked, his hair matted with perspiration.

"How you feeling?" Mel asked finally.

Nory shrugged. "Okay."

Mel waited. Then he turned to me. "You okay, Ted?"

I nodded.

Mel held the dugout fast against the rowboat.

"Get in," he ordered. Slowly we scooted down the dugout one at a time, until we could crawl over into the other boat. We sat together on the center seat.

"Look." Mel leaned forward. "I know you've got trouble at home, but there are several things you can do when the sky really dumps on you. The thing you don't want to do is take your anger out on yourself—or on somebody who didn't have a thing to do with it. I don't have to tell you the rules of the lake; you're banned from the boats for the rest of this season—both of you. If a problem comes up again, some piece of bad news, you're welcome to as much of my time as you want. Take all you need and talk my ear off. But don't you ever try something like this."

"How did you know we were out here?" I asked finally.

"The Weasels reported you missing, and when we checked around, I saw that the dugout was gone. Here, Ted, hold onto this a moment. . . ."

I crawled over and held onto the dugout while Mel climbed in it.

"Now hand me that paddle," he said.

I looked and saw that he had brought a paddle along.

"Okay," Mel said. "Head back. You row, Nory."

Nory grasped the oars and pulled. The rowboat moved down the lake toward the bend. I sat watching Mel. He dipped his paddle on one side of the dugout and then on the other. The canoe streaked swiftly, cleanly, like a knife through the water. Even in the dusk, I could see the smile spreading slowly across Mel's face.

"Hey, all riiiiight!" he murmured. "Look at her go! Look at her *go!*"

I grinned.

"Wheeee!" Mel cried softly, pleased.

When I turned my head, I could tell by the way Nory's cheeks puffed out that he was smiling, too.

The Weasels stared as we walked back into the bunk. Nory just lay down on his cot and put one arm over his eyes to shut out the questions. Nobody really knew what to say.

Mitch and Shum started a loud conversation to distract the other guys, but Sid said, "Where *were* you?"

"Just wanted to get away for a while," I told him, taking the blame with Nory.

"In Mel's canoe?" Sid insisted. They'd heard.

"It was the only one left," I told him, and realized that the room had grown very quiet. Then I added, "We got a letter from home and were sort of upset."

"Oh," said Sid.

I picked up a comic book and started reading. One by one the other guys drifted off and started talking about other things.

Nory glanced over at me. "You didn't have to *tell* them."

"You want them to go around making up stories that are even worse?" I said.

He didn't answer.

The good thing about being honest, I discovered, is that other people really do understand. I guess about half the guys in our bunkhouse come from divorced families, so they knew what it was like. They gave us space—didn't ask for details.

But I didn't *want* to belong to that half of the kids. I didn't want a weekend father who picked us up on Saturday mornings and brought us back Sunday nights. I wanted to come home from camp to two happy parents who loved each other. I wanted us to be like we used to be—everyone having a good time. If they were happy once, couldn't they be again?

The next day, Mel had a christening for his dugout canoe, and we all cheered like crazy as he took it out on the water, turned around in a wide circle, and came back. After he got out, we doused him with ginger ale. But it wasn't the same between Nory and me. I had thought, after the way he opened up the night before—after the things he'd told me—that we'd be close again. Most of the time, though, I didn't even know where Nory was.

"You've got your own friends," he said, but it wasn't like having a brother who looked out for you and you for him. It wasn't the Solomon System.

The last week of camp arrived before we knew it. Everyone seemed to be working harder at having a good time, trying to squeeze every drop of fun he could out of summer. We didn't want to miss a thing. We kept ourselves busy, rushing from field house to lake to dining hall to ball diamond as though, if we didn't run, something would get away.

I worked like crazy to finish the big drawstring bag I'd begun in leatherworking class. It was the kind of bag you could throw a bunch of clothes in and take off. I finished my basket, too, but when it was done I didn't know what I'd do with it. Did you ever try to eat beef stew from a basket? I won the archery tournament in our class, and I learned to catch fish just using a string and pole. They taught us about different kinds of bait, and I learned to snag a fish when it bit and then flip it onto the bank. *I can survive,* I thought. *I'll do okay.*

The raids at night grew wilder. There are two kinds of raids at Susquehannocks. The Killer Raid and the Kissing Raid. In the Killer Raid, one bunkhouse raids another, stripping beds and dropping shelves and generally messing things up. You need as many guys as possible for a Killer Raid—eleven Weasels, say, and two bunk counselors—armed with cans of shaving cream and talcum powder to really trash another cabin. These raids aren't officially allowed, of course, but they're usually thought up by the bunk counselors themselves. As long as things don't get out of hand, the head counselors look the other way.

A Kissing Raid, though, is something else. Even though nothing happens except a guy sitting on a girl's cot, kissing, the head counselors get nervous about Kissing Raids. One camper sneaks off to a girl's bunk, and the trick is to get there and back without Mel Kramer catching you, because it's usually Mel who's on patrol, especially during the last week.

On Wednesday night, we raided the Rapids. A Killer Raid.

"Who's got the molasses?" Shum asked. "Bernie, you got the molasses?"

"Right here," Bernie whispered as we crept along through the bushes, running from one clump to another, waiting till the coast was clear. Mitch had gone out the day before and bought four quarts of Br'er Rabbit dark. He poured it all in a paint bucket and brought a brush along.

"Keep your heads down when we cross the clearing," Shum instructed. "If they've got the door fastened, we can get in the left window. I unlocked their screen this morning."

All the lights were out in the Rapids' bunkhouse. We'd waited till eleven-thirty, so we were pretty sure they'd be asleep. The door opened without a hitch.

"Charge!" Shum whispered as he pulled the light chain. But the Rapids were gone—probably out trashing the Nighthawks. It would have been more fun if they were there, but this way we really got a chance to muck things up good. We painted molasses on everything in sight—their pillows, the chairs, the toilet seats—and then we turned off the light and took off before they could get back to catch us. Man, what luck.

At the door of our bunkhouse, however, we came to a standstill. The Rapids had been there while we were out—probably waiting for us to leave. Someone had dumped a whole wheelbarrow of sand right in the middle of our floor.

"There's sand in the sinks!" Adam yelled, going back in the cubby.

"Sand in our sneakers!" said Nory.

"Sand between our sheets," cried Joe.

Mel Kramer stuck his head in the door an hour later while we were still shoveling.

"Such diligence!" he said.

"Hey, give us a hand," Shum begged, but Mel just smiled.

"I don't understand it," he said. "Everyone's housecleaning tonight. Just passed the Rapids, and they're washing pillow cases. Keep it up, chaps. Good show!"

The next night Sid went on a Kissing Raid. "You guys cover for me," he said. "I'm going to see that short girl I was rowing with yesterday."

"Heeey, Sid! Go to it!" Shum yelled.

"Don't let Mel catch you, though," Mitch warned.

Sid turned to me because my bunk's beside his. "If anybody asks, say I got sick and went outside to throw up."

"Jeez, Sid!" I said.

Sid went out, and we all lay there in the dark wondering how far he'd get with the girl.

"Third base," predicted Joe.

"Naw," said Mitch. "Not with the bunk counselors looking on."

Sid hadn't been gone fifteen minutes before we saw a shadow outside the screen. Someone came in, but it wasn't Sid. The light flicked on, and there stood Mel Kramer.

Oh cripes! I said to myself.

"Sorry to disturb you," Mel said, moving down the row, "but I'm just making a bed check." And then he saw Sid's empty cot. "Somebody missing?"

There was no sense telling Mel that Sid was

outside throwing up. All he'd have to do would be to go out and look.

"Anybody know where he is?" Mel said.

"Think he went to take a walk," said Shum.

"No problem," said Mel. "I'll wait for him here." And with that he stretched out on Sid's cot, reached up, and pulled the light string.

Oh jeez! I thought, and rolled over.

Everyone lay still, but there wasn't a single Weasel who was sleeping.

A little later the screen door creaked, and Sid came tiptoeing in. It must not have been too easy for him to see in the dark, because he stumbled over the foot of his cot and then felt his way up the side of the bed. His hand touched Mel's arm.

"Yipes!" he said aloud.

Mel reached up and pulled the light string again. "Well, well, out for a midnight stroll, Sid?"

"Uh, sort of," said Sid. He looked around desperately, and we all tried to tell him in sign language that Mel had taken us by surprise.

Mel sat up and swung his legs over the edge of the cot.

"Since you love to get out and walk," he said, "I think I'll put you in charge of litter pickup tomorrow. You'll find the bag and stick in the office. That means you've got to cover the whole camp. Understood?"

"Yeah," said Sid.

After Mel left, all the guys teased Sid and tried to find out how far he got with the girl, but Sid wouldn't tell. That usually means that nothing happened. In fact, when a guy says he got to third base or even home, that usually means nothing happened, too.

The bunkhouse quieted down, and I drifted off to sleep. I was having one of those dreams you wish was real. I dreamed that Mom said she and Dad were staying together. She said they'd just been teasing us to see how grown-up we were. I said, "I *knew* you wouldn't really do it." Then something brushed against my face.

I tried to slip back into my dream again. But then I was conscious of Nory standing between our cots, and I opened my eyes. He was pulling on his jeans and his belt buckle tickled my hand.

"Where you going?" I asked.

"Shhh," he whispered.

I sat up on one elbow. "Who you going to see?"

Nory just smiled in the moonlight. He made his way to the screen and was gone without a sound. I reached over and moved Nory's pillow down lower in his bed, then pulled the sheet up over it.

I didn't feel so good about Nory. Maybe he

wasn't going to see a girl after all. Maybe he was going back out on the lake.

I lay there wondering what was going to happen—to him, to Mom, to Dad, to me. Nory and I had started out camp this year as close as a shoe and a sock and ended up on different feet. Nory hadn't even asked me to cover for him, like Sid had; didn't need my help. The only thing worse than not having someone you can depend on is not having someone depend on you.

I fell asleep waiting, and when I woke again it was morning. Nory was there. I knew he wouldn't tell me anything, especially with the other guys around, so I didn't ask.

There were hot cakes for breakfast—stacks of them—and even though our plates were swimming in syrup, we poured on still more. We did everything we knew we wouldn't get away with when we got back home.

"More noise! More noise!" Shum yelled, and we pounded our fists on the table. Nory moved swiftly around with his tray high in the air, delivering more hot cakes to all the tables.

And then the Willows started a chant:

> *"Marilyn Davis,*
> *In her wildest dreams. . . ."*

I stopped eating, my heart pounding:

"Nory Solomon.
Go, Nory, go!"

For a moment I felt I couldn't breathe, as though someone had punched me in the stomach. Like in a movie I saw Marilyn smile and hide her face on the shoulder of the girl next to her. Kids stood up, trying to push Marilyn and Nory together, but Nory, laughing, managed to get away and disappeared in the kitchen. I felt as though our little island was crumbling, Nory's and mine.

I shoved my plate away and sat staring at the drops of syrup that had spilled on the oilcloth. I tried to imagine Nory sitting on the edge of Marilyn's cot. I imagined it very well.

I was waiting for him outside the dining hall.

"Is that who you went to see on the Kissing Raid?" I asked, my back tense, shoulders tight.

"How'd you guess?" Nory said, handing me a sausage wrapped in tinfoil.

I threw it down. "I don't want that."

Nory looked at me. "So okay, don't eat it, then. What's wrong with you?"

I didn't know what to say, and slouched along beside him. "I just don't see why the big secret, that's all. Why didn't you tell me it was Marilyn Davis?"

Nory shrugged. "What difference does it make?"

"It makes a lot of difference," I said angrily. "She's a whole year older than you. She's going to college in September, even!"

"So?" said Nory. "I'm going to college the year after next. So what?"

"So she's practically a woman!" I shouted. "She's going to be a veterinarian. We might even end up taking Cleo to her!"

Nory stopped walking and stared at me. "Ted, what the heck is eating you? All I did was kiss her. That okay with you? I have to have your permission or something?"

I could feel my neck getting red.

"Just mind your own business from now on," Nory told me. "Get out of my life, will you?" He went on in the field house, leaving me standing there outside.

My face burned. I felt stupid and small and lost. Marilyn Davis was going to college, and I didn't even have hair under my armpits yet. I was a drip, and Nory knew it.

By lunchtime, Nory acted like nothing had happened, but we avoided each other's eyes. I was feeling so mixed-up I didn't know what I was feeling the most—hurt or angry or sad. But the more I watched Nory strutting around, holding trays over his head and flirting with Marilyn, the more I decided I wasn't going to let camp end this way for me. It wasn't enough just to put my initials on Mel's canoe. I knew I wouldn't be satisfied until I'd seen Marilyn myself one more time. I didn't care whether she was Nory's girl or not.

All the next day I stalked her, waiting for my chance, but she was always with a group of girls, or talking with Nory, or horsing around with some of the guys down by the water. And then, late in the afternoon, I found her sunbathing on the bank. She was lying on her stomach in her bathing suit and had her eyes closed.

I always think of what I should have done after it's over. I should have sat down beside her and sprinkled some cool water on her back or maybe leaned over and kissed her eyelids or something. Instead, I just stood there looking down and said, "Marilyn?"

She opened her eyes and the first thing she saw, naturally, was my feet. Two big feet in her face, practically.

Her eyes traveled up my legs, and finally she sat up and shielded her eyes. "Ted?"

I stooped down beside her on the grass. "I just wanted to say good-bye," I told her.

"I won't see you around tomorrow morning?" she asked.

"Well, everybody will be busy packing," I said.

"Oh." She watched me.

"I really wanted to give you a present," I said, and handed her the jar with Charlie in it.

She stared. "Is this . . . ?" The sun was so bright she couldn't see. She reached for her dark glasses and stared at the jar. Then she looked at me. "My gosh, Ted! Do you know . . . nobody gave me a tapeworm before—not in my entire life."

I smiled. Grinned, actually. I always have this stupid grin when I'm really trying to smile. "Well, he's yours," I said. "You can set him on your dresser or something."

"I'll keep him always," she said.

I believed her. I didn't care whether she and Nory made out or not. I didn't care how many other guys she had kissed in the Honeymoon Suite. I knew that every time Marilyn Davis looked at Charlie, for the rest of her entire life, she would think of Ted Solomon, back at Camp Susquehannocks, and that was enough for me.

It was hard to figure what Nory was thinking on the bus back home. We sat in separate seats, for one thing. He wanted to sit with some girl as far as Philadelphia, and I was stuck with Joe Reiling, who kept talking about his mother's new boyfriend. Joe's parents were divorced when he was seven.

"He's got a Porsche," Joe was saying. "Silver and black."

"You like him?" I asked.

"Oh, he's okay, I guess. Except he won't let me eat in his car. We go to McDonald's, and I have to get out."

I didn't like Mrs. Reiling's boyfriend.

After Philadelphia, when the girl got off, I

moved up and sat with Nory. It was our last chance to talk about things before we got home, but Nory pulled out a *Yes and Know* book and started playing a game with invisible ink.

I sat there, feeling miserable, while Nory turned page after page.

"Listen, Nory," I said finally, "we've got to talk before we get home—figure out what we're going to do. What if Dad won't leave and Mom decides to go? Who will do the cooking?"

Nory didn't answer.

I watched the telephone poles zipping by outside the window and tried to count all the things I could cook: fried eggs, instant oatmeal, Spanish rice, Oodles of Noodles, Burritos. . . . "I can't do pot roasts," I said aloud. "Can you do pot roasts, Nory?"

And when he didn't answer, I asked, "Do you suppose we'll get along okay if it's Mom who leaves?"

"I don't think about all the 'ifs'," Nory said. Somehow he had managed to shut that little door in his head again. He had bottled his worries up, and as long as you didn't shake him, things went along okay. I don't think I ever felt so alone in my life. Camp was over and there was nothing much at home to go back to. Worst of all, Nory and I were like strangers.

I turned my head and watched out the other

window for a while. All the way to Camp Susquehannocks, I had wondered how we'd get along without Dad: who would fix the lawnmower? Who would oil the furnace? Who would drive to the deli for bagels on Sunday morning? Who would plant the garden? Now that we were on our way home, I worried about how we'd get along without Mom. I'd stopped worrying about that little kid in the Muskrats' bunkhouse, though. Both Jake's parents had come to pick him up, and they'd all walked to the parking lot with their arms around each other. It made me feel hollow inside.

When we pulled into the depot in Washington, I saw Dad leaning against the hood of the Buick, waiting. He looked tan and maybe a little older, but he gave us a big smile and hugged us hard.

"Gosh, it's sure good to have you back," he said. "Ted, you've grown another two inches, I swear it." And as we drove home, he bombarded us with questions: "Any trouble with poison ivy this year?" "The girls just as pretty, Nory?" "What was the fishing like?" He hit every subject in the book except what was happening between him and Mom. And suddenly I had this horrible thought: maybe neither Mom or Dad was moving out. Maybe things were going to go right on the way they'd been lately, forever and ever: Mom not speaking to Dad; Dad not sleeping with Mom; the silences at meal time; the tension; the stares. I sucked in my breath and pressed against the back of the seat.

As we pulled in the driveway, I saw Mom in the doorway waiting for us, smiling. And suddenly I remembered Cleo.

"Hey! Where's Cleo?" I asked Dad.

"Listen, Ted, there's been some trouble." I caught Dad's eyes in the rearview mirror and knew he was stalling.

I started scrambling over Nory's legs there in the back seat to get to the door. "What happened?" I shouted. "What's happened to Cleo?" I pushed the door open and tumbled out.

"There was a fight," Dad said. "That big dog up the street—Brute—was down here one day when Cleo was out and attacked. She's okay now—the wounds are healing nicely—but for a while there it was touch and go."

I rushed up the steps, pushing past Mom—shoving her out of the way, almost. Cleo was limping slowly through the living room toward me, one hind leg in a cast, a big bare patch on her side with an ugly raggedy scar, her left eye swollen and oozing.

"Cleo!" I whispered, and knelt down, wrapping my arms gently about her. She feebly licked my cheek.

"What was Cleo doing out where Brute could get to her?" I yelled angrily as Dad came inside carrying our bags. “Why wasn’t someone with her?”

Mom came over and sat down on the hassock beside me. “We just let her out for a little while one morning, honey. We certainly didn’t know that Brute was around. We called the police, of course, and they’ve issued a warning to the owner. . . . ”

“When you have dogs, you have to be responsible!” I shouted. “You shouldn’t have let her out.”

Mom and Dad just stared at me. Nory, too. He patted Cleo on the head and then walked over to the mantel to sort his mail.

I hadn’t even said hello to Mom. Hadn’t even hugged her. But I wasn’t thinking of that. “People just go on getting dogs and never worrying about what’s going to happen to them,” I went on shouting. “They treat them nice when they’re puppies, and then just don’t care about them anymore.”

“Oh, Ted,” said Mom, and her face looked all twisted out of shape. “That’s not true. We didn’t know—”

“You have to think about things before they happen,” I insisted. “If you can’t take care of a dog right, then don’t have dogs.”

I stopped, breathing hard. Mom’s face seemed twisted even more. Dad looked grave. I stooped down and gently picked Cleo up and took her to my room—gentle Cleo, who had never been in a fight before. I felt as though another chunk of my island had fallen off. I had lost something else I had learned to count on.

Mom and Dad were both trying hard to keep our homecoming pleasant, I realized later. Mom had a good dinner prepared, and even though she and Dad didn't say much to each other, they were polite and didn't bang things around. Each of them had saved up bits of news to tell us.

"Big fire over on Howard Avenue while you were gone," Dad said. "An antique store and a cabinet shop, I think. You could see the flames from our porch."

"John Jennings called while you were gone, Ted," Mom said next. "He says that he and his dad are planning their raft trip for a Saturday in September and hope you can come along. I said you'd call."

So I tried to be civil, too. I told them about the Killer Raid at camp, and Nory told about being a waiter, and we both said how nice it was that Grandma could come up on Visiting Day.

"She's coming down next weekend," Mom said. "I thought you'd like that."

Dad took us out to see his garden after dinner and announced that the Supersonics were ahead of the Jetstars by seven. Then Nory and I went upstairs to unpack. We had barely opened our bags when Mom came to the doorway, holding her glass of iced tea.

"I thought I ought to say something about next year," she began cautiously. "We *hope* we can still send you to camp, but we can't promise. If we're going to be running two different households, money will be very tight. We'll have to have another car—more furniture, I suppose, so . . . well, I just don't want you to get your hopes up. Anything you boys can do to help earn a little will be appreciated."

I looked up. "So what's going to happen, Mom? Who's moving out?"

"It's still up in the air," she said. She waited. "How do you boys feel about it? Any ideas on the subject?"

I looked at Nory. *Speak, Nory, for Pete's sake,* I thought. But when he didn't, I said, "No, we don't have any ideas about it, so just don't ask us, okay?"

"Okay, Ted, okay," Mom said quietly, and went back downstairs.

I would have felt better if Nory had done the talking. He didn't say a word, either to Mom or to me.

That evening I felt guilty about the way I'd been treating Mom, so just before I went to bed, I went in the living room where she was reading and gave her a quick hug.

"Good night," I said.

She took hold of my arm and pulled me gently

down beside her. "You're angry with me, Ted. I can tell. And I don't think it's just over Cleo."

I sat beside her, rubbing my thumbs together, staring down at them. "Of course it's not just over Cleo," I told her. "I don't like my life pulled apart, that's what. I don't like you and Dad splitting up."

"I don't either," she said. "But a lot of things happen that we don't like, and somehow we have to learn to accept them."

I knew that if I was ever going to ask Mom what was wrong between her and Dad—what was *really* wrong—now was the time to ask it. But I didn't. I was afraid that it might hurt too much to know—that it would start me thinking about "if onlys" again.

"But you're right," Mom went on. "It's not fair for Gene and me to involve you boys in the decision." She put one arm around my shoulder, and I didn't pull away. "The problem isn't who gets the car or the garden or even the house; it's who gets to live with you boys. That's the part we can't agree on. But it's our problem, not yours. Don't you ever doubt that we love you."

I didn't. I liked the warmth of her arm around my shoulder. It was a lot harder to think about loving feelings than it was to be angry—a lot easier to yell and kick a chair than to admit that I wanted both Mom and Dad.

I remembered when I was small, how Dad used to sit on one side of me and Mom on the other, and then they'd hug, with me squished in the middle. *A snuggle sandwich,* Dad used to call it. I couldn't believe how much I wanted that now.

16

The fighting began the next day—not the beating-up kind, but the fighting with words. It stopped at the dinner table when Nory and I sat down and started again as soon as we left the kitchen. It went on all Monday evening and into Tuesday—mostly in the den, with the door closed.

Sometimes I could hear my name mentioned, or Nory's, but usually it was about things I didn't understand.

"Did *I* ask for that?" I heard Mom yell once as I walked by the door. "Carry the boys on your policy, and I'll take out health insurance at work. The less we have to do with each other, Gene, the better." Her voice was shrill. Ugly.

Or Dad would say something like, "It doesn't concern me in the least. You've been doing just what you want for a long time now." His voice was cold. Unloving.

Sometimes it seemed as though they were almost shouting, and when that happened, I didn't even *want* to know what they were arguing about. I'd go upstairs and take Cleo with me, shutting the door. Then I'd lie on my bed and read Asterix comics or look through Nory's yearbook again.

There was something about his yearbook that I liked—all those pictures of people smiling—pictures of students making a snowman that looked like the principal, or a row of pom-pom girls cheering. No matter what else happened to you, you could always look in your yearbook and remember that you were in the concert band or the spring play or the photography club and nobody could take that away. There you were on stage, smiling, and if you ever wondered later how you felt back then, you could find the picture that proved you were happy.

Nory kept himself busy. He used all his energy rushing from one thing to another and didn't have time left for worrying. When I woke up in the mornings, Nory was already gone—to the tennis court, then the track, then the pool. The worse the fighting got between Mom and Dad, the more Nory was gone.

Aunt Sheila called one afternoon.

"Hi, dear," she said. "Busy?"

"No," I told her. "Everyone's out."

"Well, my gosh! I certainly think we ought to be able to find something for you to do," she said. "I'm just sitting here wondering if you and Nory could come over this evening for a cookout. David has to go somewhere later, of course, but the three of us could take in a movie or something."

It was the first time in the four years that Uncle David and Aunt Sheila had lived in Washington that she had asked Nory and me over for dinner—alone. I panicked. I just knew that if Nory and I went over there, we'd end up adopted or something.

"Well . . . I don't think so," I said. "We're sort of busy."

There was silence from the other end. Then, "I thought you said you weren't."

"Well, I mean . . . I'm not busy at the moment, but I will be later, and Nory's not here . . . ."

"I just thought you might like to get away from things for a while."

That scared me even more.

"What things?" I asked, playing dumb.

She didn't answer. I waited.

Finally she said, "Well, Ted, maybe we can make it some other time."

"Sure," I said. "Thanks anyway."

On Wednesday, I was looking through the yearbook again when Nory dashed in to pick up his swim trunks.

"Nory," I said, pointing to one of the scribbled paragraphs on the inside cover. "Did you know that Mickey Johnson got hold of your book? Did you see what she *wrote*?"

Nory just leaned toward the mirror and examined a pimple on his chin. I bet he hadn't seen the note, so I read it aloud, " 'To my one and only. Stay as sweet as you are, Nory. History with you was absolutely fantastic. Hope we can get some classes together next year. Your warm fuzzy, Mickey Johnson.' "

Nory didn't even blink, and then I realized he'd already seen it. *Asked* her to write it, even.

"Why'd you let her write this goopy stuff?" I said disgustedly. "Now you have to look at it the rest of your life."

"Oh, grow up, Ted," Nory said, and pulled on a tee shirt.

I stomped across the room and slammed the yearbook back on the shelf. And then I happened to look out the window and there, on the street below, was Mickey Johnson in her dad's Honda, waiting for Nory.

"She can *drive*?" I asked in astonishment.

"Yeah. Got her license while I was at camp."

I couldn't stand it anymore. "So go ahead and

marry her!" I screeched. "Go your whole life married to someone named Mickey, for Pete's sake!"

But Nory was already going downstairs, and the screen door slammed. He jumped in the Honda, and the car pulled away.

I sat on the bed a long time, thinking things over. I didn't like what was happening to Nory and me. It wasn't the Solomon System anymore, it was each guy for himself. But Nory was right; I was acting sort of dumb. About Marilyn. About Mickey.

I wanted to prove that I *was* growing up, that I could do something besides sit here making wisecracks. I'd surprise Nory by getting a job while he was out running around with Mickey. We had to have money if we were going to make it back to camp next summer.

The problem was I'd never really looked for work before. I got the paper and turned the pages of the want-ads, past furniture for sale and houses for rent to a column called "business opportunities."

"Coin-operated laundry," an advertisement read, and gave a phone number. I figured I could put clothes in a washing machine, so I dialed the number and said I was interested in the ad. The man said he was asking twenty thousand. I didn't understand.

"The job pays twenty-thousand?" I asked.

"What are you talking about?" the man said. "I'm selling the place, what do you think?"

I told him I had the wrong number. Then I went back to the newspaper and found three pages of "Help Wanted."

I spread the papers out on the floor of our room. Unfortunately none of the things I had learned at camp were listed. No ads for a carver of dugout canoes No archery experts. No cubby cleaners. I circled all the ones that sounded possible or interesting: *desk clerk; disc jockey; dog groomer; lifeguard; sign painter; telephone solicitor; waiter. . . .*

I dialed the number for dog-groomer.

"Atwell's Dog Grooming," a woman answered.

"Hello," I said, and swallowed. "I'm calling about that job." I tried to make my voice sound lower, but it got all foggy.

"Experience?"

"Oh, yes, I've had a lot of experience," I told her.

"How old are you?"

"Thirteen."

She hung up. She didn't even say good-bye.

I wasn't getting very far.

John Jennings rode by on Friday.

"What about the raft trip?" he asked. "You could bring your dad too, if you want."

"Well . . . ." In a way I wanted to go. In a way I didn't. He hadn't invited Nory, for one thing, and

I didn't usually go many places without Nory. "Could I let you know later?" I asked.

"Sure," he said. "But we've got to make reservations."

"I'll call you in a few days," I said.

The best thing about Friday was that Grandma came down from Baltimore for the weekend. It had been a long time since she'd come on a Friday, because she usually spends Sabbath at home. We don't do much on Sabbath, but when Grandma Rose is here, Mom lights the candles and Dad says a blessing and then we pass around a loaf of bread and all break off a little piece. You'd be surprised how happy this makes Grandma.

But on this particular Friday, Mom didn't smile when she lit the candles and Dad merely mumbled the blessing.

"Shabbat Shalom," said Grandma, as the bread went around. She sat back and looked at us. "Well!" she said at last. "We are sitting shiva, maybe?" (Mourning the dead, she meant.) She was trying to make a joke, but it didn't work. I knew what Grandma was thinking about us, anyway. I heard her tell Mom once. She said maybe there wouldn't be all this marriage trouble if we were better Jews and went to synagogue, and Mom told her that it was a little more complicated than that.

Grandma focussed on Nory and me. "So how

are the campers? Didn't get fat, I see, and that's good."

Neither Nory or I could think of anything to say.

Mom dished up the soup and passed the bowls around. "We're just not feeling very peppy, Mother," she said.

"That's obvious," Grandma said, but added cheerfully, "So I'll talk and you listen." She laughed, and Nory and I smiled, but Mom and Dad just sat clinking their spoons against the sides of their bowls as they ate, and after a while even Grandma didn't feel like talking.

"We'll do the dishes," she said to Mom after dessert. "You two go on, now. The boys and I will clean up."

She didn't really know what she was saying. As soon as Mom and Dad left the table, they went down to the den and closed the door, the way they had every evening since Nory and I got home.

"They're writing letters or what?" Grandma asked, pausing uncertainly in the doorway.

"Sorting through papers and stuff," Nory told her.

"Trying to decide who leaves and who gets to stay," I added.

"Oy vey," Grandma murmured under her breath, and her face clouded over, every wrinkle a little deeper.

"Listen, Grandma," I said suddenly, "if they can't decide and it goes to court and the judge gives us to Uncle David and Aunt Sheila, can we come and live with you instead?"

Grandma turned slowly around and looked at me intently. "Such a lot of 'ifs,' " she said. "If it comes to that, and I am doubting very much, we will see what's best." She tied an apron around her waist and moved toward the sink. "Now," she said, "I will sing."

Grandma loves to sing while she works. She always tells us about a song first, because we don't understand the language. It's funny about Grandma's songs—no matter how the melody starts out, it always changes somewhere in the middle. If it starts out sad, you know it will get happy later on. And if it starts out happy, you know it will get mournful. I asked her about it once, why her songs are like that, and she said because life is like that: bittersweet.

"Now this one," she said, rinsing each plate as I handed it to her, "is called *Vos Villstu,* and it's between a girl and her mother. The mother says what kind of man does the daughter want to marry, eh? A shoemaker? No. A tailor? No. A rabbi, even? No. Not even a *rabbi*? What *does* she want? She wants a *klezmer,* a musician."

I kept on bringing the plates one at a time, then the wine goblets, to make it last longer. Nory stacked all the silverware by the sink. It was nice to hear Grandma's songs in our kitchen—good to have music drowning out the voices back in the den. Even Cleo seemed happy. She lay in one corner, panting, watching us with a dog's good humor.

"And this one," said Grandma, starting the next song, "is about a quarrel. 'Let's make up,' says the woman. 'Let's be pleasant to each other. I have for you tea and oranges'—" Grandma stopped suddenly. "No, I think I won't sing that one." She frowned and reached for the soup kettle.

"Sing the one about the old aunt who wasn't invited to the wedding but went anyway," said Nory.

"Ah, that's a good one," said Grandma Rose, and her rich voice filled the kitchen again. Nory and I joined in the chorus. Mostly we do that to tease Cleo. She's not used to us singing—we probably sound terrible—and she always gets to her feet, like it's the national anthem or something. By the time the dishes were done, we were all laughing.

But the quarreling went on well into the night, which really surprised me. It was the first time I could ever remember Mom and Dad arguing so furiously when Grandma Rose was around. None of us could hear what they were actually saying. Just an exclamation now and then, or the thud of Dad's foot on the floor. I knew that Grandma could hear them too from her bedroom next to ours. Once

I sat up, thinking maybe I'd go in to her, just to talk, but I didn't.

I knew Nory wasn't sleeping either. Nobody could sleep with all that yelling going on. The tension in our house was like fog—you could almost see it, breathe it, but you couldn't actually get hold of it. Finally he rose up on one elbow.

"My god," he said. "Don't they ever sleep?"

"I never thought they'd be like this with Grandma here," I told him.

He laid back down and sighed, and we watched the changing pattern of light on the ceiling as the cars drove by. "Nory," I said finally, glad that he was talking. "Do you remember the snuggle sandwich?" I don't know why I asked him that. It was embarrassing, really, but it just came out.

He was quiet for a long time. Just when I thought he wasn't going to answer, he said, "Yeah. I'd forgotten all about it. But that was a long time ago—a million years, maybe."

I heard Mom coming up to bed finally. Even her footsteps, soft as they were, sounded tired—a pause between each one. We heard her pick up the plastic cup in the bathroom, but it fell out of her hands and rolled clattering around in the sink. A lonely sound. Then she went down the hall to the bedroom at the end and closed the door.

The next morning at breakfast, Dad and Mom were there. It was strange seeing them at breakfast together, especially on a Saturday. Their eyes were red-rimmed, and somehow I knew they had reached a decision. The fight had gone out of them. They were exhausted.

Grandma clucked disapprovingly as she poured their coffee. "Just look at you! Why get up? Why aren't you sleeping? Here, Elaine, sit down and I'll do the eggs." She busied herself at the stove, and Mom seemed glad to have somebody fuss over her.

Nory and I silently ate our toast, sharing the comics between us. And then, right in the middle of Garfield, I heard Dad say, "Elaine and I have come to a decision, boys, and I guess this is as good a time as any to announce it."

"I'll just go up and make my bed," Grandma said hastily, starting to take off her apron, but Mom stopped her.

"You stay here, Mother," she said. "You're family, too."

Grandma lowered herself down on the telephone stool next to the wall, her hands folded in her lap, motionless.

"It's been almost impossible for Elaine and me to come to a decision about who moves out," Dad said. "Naturally, neither of us wants to be the absent parent, missing out on your growing up."

They're going to stay together! I thought.

"We finally worked out a plan," Dad went on.

"It's not perfect, by any means, but it's the only solution we could think of."

They're separating, I told myself.

Dad's face seemed to be growing older by the second. "We realize it hasn't been fair for us to try to involve you in the decision, so we went ahead and made it ourselves. I'm going to leave—rent an apartment somewhere—and let one of you boys live with me for a while. Ted, we thought maybe you'd like to stay with me the first year, and then you and Nory can switch."

I didn't move. I couldn't believe him. I felt that the rest of my island, the little bit that was left, had just broken up into a thousand pieces and was drifting out to sea.

"We won't be far," Dad told us. "I'll try to find a place close enough that you boys can get together, go to the same school and all. But this way neither Elaine nor I has to come home to an empty house, and each of you boys will have a parent all to yourself. Perhaps we'll feel even closer to each other than we do now."

I couldn't even blink my eyes. I sat staring past Mom, who was watching me intently, to Grandma, who seemed to have frozen there on the telephone stool like a little ceramic woman. She looked old, too, far too old to have Nory and me move in with her.

"It might seem strange at first," Mom said

quickly, "but it does seem a more fair arrangement."

I just couldn't talk. My tongue wouldn't move. Of the four of us there at the table, only Nory kept eating. His hand moved up and down from plate to mouth like a wind-up toy, teeth chewing, eyes on the wall ahead. *He doesn't care!* I thought, and that hurt the most of all.

"I'd like to know how you fellas feel about it," Dad said, surprised at the way Nory was acting. "This is a pretty big change in living arrangements, I know . . . ."

Nory got up, pushed his chair in, and started upstairs.

"Nory," Dad called after him. "Come on, now. Let's talk about this." But we heard Nory's footsteps on the floor overhead.

"Well," Dad said, "I guess it's going to take some getting used to." He turned to me. "I'm going to check the paper today and do some calling. Thought I might go out tomorrow and look for a place. You can come with me if you want; help me pick something."

I nodded woodenly.

I was thinking about a building we passed once in Bethesda, a long time ago, called the Baptist Home for Children. Before I started worrying about Mom and Dad divorcing, I worried about them dying, and about what would happen to Nory and me if they did. Then we passed that building and Dad said it was probably an orphanage, and I tried to memorize how we got back to Kensington from there. I wanted to know, see, that if Nory and I ever had to, we could get on our bikes and ride over. I figured they'd take any little kids who were unlucky enough to be orphans, Jewish or not. Now I wished there was some place like that I could run off to.

Mom went down in the basement to do the laundry, and Dad went back to the den. Slowly Grandma got off her stool. She reached across the table with her speckled hand and grabbed mine, holding it hard.

"Ted," she said, "do you know the story of King Solomon?"

I couldn't believe what Dad had said. I couldn't believe that Nory would just go off and not say anything. I couldn't believe that Mom was down in the basement doing laundry, as though nothing had happened. And now I couldn't believe that, after all of this, Grandma was going to tell me a story!

She kept squeezing my hand.

"He was a wise king, that Solomon. And one day two women came to him, bringing a boy, and each said that she was his mother. So what does a big king know about mothers, eh? You know what Solomon said? He said, 'Cut the boy in half and give a part to each woman.' "

I blinked. "Did they?"

"No. That old king was a brain and a half, I tell you. Because the real mother, the true mother, said she would rather have the other woman take the boy than tear him apart. And when King Solomon heard that, he said, 'Give the child to that woman, for she is the true mother.' "

Grandma put both hands on top of mine. "They are hurting so inside themselves, Ted, that they just don't realize how much they are hurting you."

Dad's footsteps sounded again in the hallway, and Grandma turned toward the dishes in the sink. As Dad was pouring more coffee, Nory came downstairs.

"You going to use the car today, Dad?" he asked. Just like that. Real cool.

"Probably not. I think I'll save the apartment hunting for tomorrow. You want to use it?"

"Thought Ted and I would go to the pool."

I looked at Nory. I couldn't figure him out. Everything was caving in around us, and he decides to go swimming. But I was so glad to be invited I didn't care. I wanted Nory and me to be like we were before. I wanted us to be a team.

"Sure. Go on," Dad said, puzzled.

"Get your suit and towel," Nory told me.

When we were in the car, though, I couldn't hold back any longer. Tears formed in the corners of my eyes, but I just didn't care. "I don't want to move out, Nory," I gulped.

"I know," Nory said, and backed the Buick down the drive.

We went up Kensington Parkway toward Connecticut and stopped at the light. The tears kept coming.

"I never thought they'd do this," I said. "I never thought they'd split *us* up."

Nory didn't answer. He turned on the radio, then turned it off. He reached out the window and adjusted the side mirror. The light switched to green, and the Buick moved forward. But we turned right, not left.

I looked over at Nory. "The pool's the other way," I told him.

"Yeah, I know," he said, and a minute later pulled up the ramp to the Beltway.

I held onto the edge of the seat as Nory curved around the ramp. At the top, tractor trailers whooshed by. Nory waited, then darted out suddenly into the right lane. There we were—on Route 495. I didn't know where we were going, but it sure felt good.

"Where we going, Nory?" I asked finally. He was leaning forward, his back not even touching the seat, hands gripping the wheel hard. I could tell by the white of his knuckles.

"Frederick," he said.

I looked over at him. *"Frederick?* Where's that?"

"North on Two Seventy," Nory told me, and I knew he had figured it all out.

I didn't take my eyes off him. "What are we going to do in Frederick?"

"Go live with Mel," he said.

The shock of it, the thrill, and the awfulness of running away made goosebumps on my arms. The Solomon System was working again. I sort of wished Nory had told me in advance, though, because I hadn't brought anything along. After all the work I did on that drawstring bag in the leather-working class, it would have been nice to stuff some clothes in it and throw it in the car. But at least we were doing something. We were really running away. And it made more sense to go to Frederick than to live in a cave somewhere. At least Mel could cook.

"How long will it take to get there?" I asked.

"An hour, maybe."

"Mel know we're coming?"

"No."

I tried to picture Mel Kramer's face when we told him. *Hi, Mel. Thought we'd come up here and live with you. Got our bathing suits right there in the back seat.*

"I suppose he's got room for us," I said, trying to think of a reason why the whole thing might work. "We can help out on his farm and everything."

"Yeah," said Nory. He started to pass a car, then pulled back as a pickup sped by him.

"Jeez, Nory!" I cried. "Watch it! Don't go so fast."

Nory slowed down a little. I tugged on my seat belt and tightened it, frowning at Nory. "You got Mel's address?"

"We'll find it."

I watched the Saturday traffic whiz by us on the left. A sign loomed up: 270 NEXT RIGHT. Nory followed the bend at the exit, waited for a break in traffic, and then pulled onto the freeway, heading north. I settled back in the seat. Wide stretches of farmland appeared outside the window already.

It was Nory, strangely, who felt like talking now.

"It's their turn," he said bitterly. "Let *them* worry for a while. Let *them* wonder what's going to happen. All they care about is how *they're* going to feel coming home to an empty house. Did they ever ask each other how *we're* going to feel coming home after school with nobody there?"

Nory cared. He really did. All this time he'd pretended I didn't mean anything to him anymore, but I did. I thought of Grandma's story about King Solomon. "Next they'll even want to divide up Cleo," I said. "Each take half."

"Yeah, do they ever think of her?" Nory said.

"It's not just Mom's and Dad's problem—we're all mixed up in it—you, me, Cleo, Grandma. . . ." He was saying all the things I'd been thinking all this time; he was also driving too fast again.

"Slow down, Nory ," I said.

He lifted his foot off the gas, but a few minutes later the speedometer was climbing.

"All that talk about loving us so much, all that talk about caring—"

"Slow down, Nory," I said.

He didn't even hear me.

"You know what I wanted to do at breakfast this morning?" he said, and his voice was loud. "I just wanted to take my arm and sweep everything off the table—cream, sugar, eggs—everything off into their laps. Just push all the stuff off and walk out."

The Buick swung around a station wagon, tailgated a Mercedes, and then swerved back in the right lane again. We were at least fifteen miles over the speed limit. My heart pounded against the wall of my chest. I was really scared.

"Nory," I cried, "you're going too fast. You'll get a ticket."

"To hell with them!" Nory yelled, going even faster. He brought his left foot down hard against the floorboard and pushed down even more on the gas with the right.

"Police car, Nory!" I hollered. "Pull over!"

Nory lifted his foot off the gas and began to brake.

"Where?"

"Coming up. Slow down. Pull over on the shoulder."

Nory edged his way over, the car going slower and slower, until finally we moved off onto the shoulder, rolled a way, and then stopped.

"Where?" Nory said again.

I was already unbuckling my seat belt. I opened the door on my side and jumped out. There wasn't any police car.

"Go on, Nory," I yelled angrily, my heart still pounding. "Go on and kill yourself! *You're* the one who doesn't care. You're so mad at Mom and Dad you'll kill both of us to get even."

I could feel the blood throbbing in my neck. Faces stared at us from passing cars, but they were only a blur. Nory slid over on my side of the car, swung his legs out, and sat with elbows on his knees, head down, breathing hard.

"Mom and Dad make their grand announcement, and what do you do?" I went on. "Do you tell them it's just not right? Do you tell them we're a team? No, you don't say a darn word!" I wasn't really being fair to Nory, because I hadn't said a word either, but this time I was really mad. "Then you come out here and scare *me* half to death, trying to smear us both all over the highway."

Nory took a deep breath.

"I'm sorry, Ted," he said. "It's just like Mel said—I'm taking it out on us. Come on. Get in. I'll be careful."

I watched him warily. "You got anymore to say, you say it now," I insisted.

"It's over," Nory said. "For now, anyway."

"You'll drive the speed limit? Promise?"

"Yes. Come on."

Nory slid back over and I got in. We buckled up again. Nory waited till there was a clean break in traffic, then carefully pulled out. He drove cautiously the rest of the way to Frederick.

Neither of us knew Mel's address. We stopped at a phone booth and looked up his name in the directory. We copied down the address and went to a grocery to ask directions. The man said it was out in the country and drew us a map on a paper sack.

We drove from one end of the road to the other, but couldn't find Mel's box and had to drive it again. The sky had clouded over and big splotches of rain splattered on the windshield, but then it passed and the sun came out. Finally, on the second trip, I saw a rusty mailbox with "Kramer" on the side, and we turned up the long dirt drive.

It didn't look like much of a farm—a sort of

ramshackle barn and a tractor half-covered with vines. The house needed paint, but we could tell that someone lived in it. There was an old Chevy parked under a beech tree, so we pulled up beside it.

"You do the talking, Nory," I said.

We both got out and walked around the yard, hoping Mel would see us and come to the door. Finally Nory went up to the screen and knocked. No answer.

"Hey, Mel!" he yelled.

The breeze fluttered a loose shingle on the side of the house.

Then we saw someone coming around the barn. It was a man about Mel's size, but it wasn't Mel.

"Hello," he called, walking over.

"Mel around?" Nory asked.

The man put down his bucket and wiped his forehead. "He know you were coming?" he asked. "Went to Jersey City over the weekend to see a lady friend."

I felt all the excitement ebb away, like a leak in the soles of my feet. Nory's shoulders sagged.

"Be back Monday or Tuesday, I figure," the man went on. "I just come over here twice a day to do the chores." He studied us. "Where you know Mel from? Camp?"

"Yeah," said Nory.

"Where you live?"

"Kensington."

"Just out driving around, huh?"

Nory paused. "Yeah, that's all." I knew then that Nory wasn't going to ask if we could stay. I knew that the long drive to Frederick had been for nothing.

"Well, sorry you missed Mel." The hired man wiped his hands on his overalls, went in the house, and came back out with two cans of 7-Up. He handed them to us. "You sit here and refresh yourselves before you head back." He locked the door after him. "Yep. Mel will be sorry he missed you, but he's got this lady friend. Wouldn't surprise me a bit they end up getting married." He got in the old battered Chevy, waved, and drove off.

"What do we do now, Nory?" I asked.

"Rats!" was all Nory said. He sat down on the doorstep and I flopped down beside him.

Nory's silence began to get to me—the way he was pulling back inside himself again. He got me all the way out here, doggone it, and I wanted to see some action. I wanted to hear a plan.

"What are we going to do, Nory?" I said again, louder.

Nory swallowed the rest of his drink and flattened the can between his palms. "Go home, I guess. What else?"

I felt as though the 7-Up was rising in my

throat, filling my mouth and nose. Fizzing out my ears, even. I felt like a thermometer that's been set in hot water, and mercury was pushing against the top of my head.

"No!" I yelled, jumping up and kicking the step hard. "You can't *do* that, Nory! We came all the way up here for a reason!"

Nory shrugged. "We came up here to live with Mel, and he's not home."

"Then we'll go somewhere else!"

Nory just sighed. "It was probably a dumb idea."

"It was *not*!" I yelled. "You're chickening out! I thought we were tired of being pulled apart, of always being in the middle! I thought we were going to stay up here until Mom and Dad worked things out."

"Yeah?" Nory said. "You'll be an old man, Ted."

"*You're* the old man!" I bellowed, kicking the step again—so hard that my toes hurt inside my sneakers. "You know what you're afraid of? You're afraid we can't do it—live off by ourselves."

"Oh, for Pete's sake, Ted." Nory rubbed his forehead.

"Scaredy!" I shot back. "You're scared of Dad, aren't you? Scared of what he'll say."

"Bug off."

"Mud-face!" I taunted, furious. "You don't have any guts, Nory! You're chicken!"

Nory gave me a dirty look and stood up. "Well, I'm going home."

"*Go* home!" I shrieked at him. "Get out of here! Get your mud face out of here. It makes me sick!"

"Come on, Ted. . . ."

"No!" My voice cracked with rage. "There's nothing to go home *for*. I hate you, Nory! It's all over with us."

"You're a jerk," said Nory.

"You're a worse one!" I was surprised to discover I was crying. I was crying and screaming at the same time. "Go home and make out with Mickey! That's all you want to do, anyway."

"Oh, shut up." Nory turned and started for the car. I ran after him and kicked my 7-Up can. It almost hit his ear. "Go home, stink-hole!" I bellowed, the tears streaming down my face. "Get out of here mud-face, bald-legs, stink-hole."

Nory turned and stared at me, then got in the car and slammed the door hard. He turned the car around, tires spinning, and took off.

I stood in the clearing, breathing hard. My heart was throbbing so hard I could hear it in my ears. I saw the car stop when it reached the end of the lane, then turn right and keep going.

I sat down on the stoop, wiping my arm across my eyes. It was as though I had been separated from everyone on earth—from Mom, from Dad, from Grandma, from Mel, and now Nory. It was all over now, The Solomon System. Just like blowing out the flame on a candle.

Mel's place was awfully quiet. After a while I began to wonder what time it was, and what I was going to do after it got dark. I sure wasn't going to try to get in Mel's house, even though he probably wouldn't mind. Somehow I was going to get along out here by myself. I stood up and walked to the barn.

There was a shed on one side with the roof caved in, and birds were flying in and out. They dived at me when I got near. I went on around to the barn entrance.

It was dark inside, darker than a barn is supposed to be in daylight, I think. It smelled old. There was hay in one corner, and it smelled old too. A hen up in the loft flapped her wings and cackled, and then came fluttering down, clucking at me, and pecked at the dirt floor. A cow at the far end of the barn went on munching hay.

I crawled up to where the hen had been and found three eggs. One of them was warm and the other two smelled funny. I decided I would boil the fresh egg for supper and get some milk from the cow. Outside, I looked around for a tin can to boil some water in, but by the time I'd gathered wood, I realized that the one thing I hadn't learned at camp was how to make a fire without matches. I didn't care, though. I wasn't hungry.

Sitting on the front stoop again, I leaned against the screen and thought how cruddy life was. What a mess Mom and Dad had made of things! How could they have loved each other so much once and then become enemies over the last few years? How did that happen unless they let it happen? And then I thought of Nory and me, and how long we'd been a team and how, in one summer, but mostly in the space of a single afternoon, we'd blown it sky-high.

I sucked in my breath. Trouble had been building up all summer, I told myself—that's why it happened: Nory not talking; Nory fooling around with Marilyn; Nory fooling around with Mickey; Nory keeping secrets. . . . And then I thought of the way I'd been bugging him, poking my nose in his business, making wisecracks. . . .

It seemed as though I'd been there on the doorstep for several hours, and yet I knew I hadn't. I wondered what would happen first—the hired man would come back to milk the cow or Dad would drive up to get me. *Nory should be home,* I thought. I could picture him standing in the living room, telling Dad what happened. I could see Dad scowling, grabbing the keys out of Nory's hand, and heading outside to the car.

So take off, I told myself. *Clear out. Hitchhike to Pennsylvania or something.* But the more I thought about how there wasn't much at home to go back to, the more I realized there wasn't much to stick around for out here, either. If I was going to be miserable, I might just as well be miserable in my own home with hot and cold running water. The more I stared at the egg in my hand, the more I didn't want it.

Then I saw our car far down the road. It was moving slowly, the way they do when they're about to turn in. It turned and started up the drive. My heart began pounding again. Dad would be furious. Absolutely wild. I stared down at my feet. The car stopped and the door opened. When I looked up, I was looking at Nory.

"Listen, Ted," he said. "If you don't come, there's not much for me to go back for either. Let's go home."

That's the way Nory is sometimes. He could have grabbed my arm and punched me. He could have called me fish face and said my feet stunk. Instead, he let me know he missed me. I stood up and walked to the car.

We didn't say too much on the way back. Hardly a word, in fact. I wondered if Nory had driven all the way to Kensington and then turned around again and come for me. But I didn't ask. At one point, he looked over and saw the egg in my hand. He stared at it a moment, then put one hand on my shoulder and left it there for a while.

We reached home and pulled in the drive. The concrete had a damp, clean look, and the air was fresher, cooler, than when we left. I could hear Cleo barking the way she does when either Nory or I come home. Then the screen door flew open, and first Dad, then Mom and Grandma, appeared in the doorway.

Mom just stood there with one hand to her throat, and then she moved over to the porch railing and sat down, as though her legs had given out.

"Bless the Lord," said Grandma Rose.

I couldn't understand why they were so upset. We've stayed at the pool all day lots of times.

Dad didn't say anything for a moment, then he started down the steps.

"Where the heck have you been?"

Nory and I got out.

"I . . . I asked if I could use the car," said Nory. "It's only five-thirty."

"And where did you say you were going?"

"The pool," said Nory.

"Sha!" said Grandma reproachfully. "You'd lie, Nory?"

He dropped his eyes. "How'd you find out?"

"You'll notice while we're talking that the streets are wet, maybe?" said Grandma Rose. "You'll notice one thing more, that there are puddles?"

"It rained," said Mom, the color coming back to her face. "That's how we found out."

It still didn't make sense. It rains lots of times when we're at the pool, and we just stand under the shelter till it's over.

"A girl called for you, Nory," Dad explained. "We told her you went to the pool. She said she'd just come from there—that she left when it started to rain—and you hadn't been there at all."

Mickey Johnson, I thought. *Wouldn't you know!*

"Finally," Mother said, "we called some of your friends, but no one had seen you. That's when we called the police."

"I didn't figure you'd miss us that soon," said Nory.

"In that case, worry a little," Grandma scolded. "It's not so terrible to call home, is it? Not so awful to tell your mother where you are?"

"Let's go inside," said Dad.

I never thought that Grandma would be against us, too. By the time we got in the living room, though, her face had softened. She took a chair off in the dining room, the way she does when she wants to show that she's not going to interfere in family business, but close enough to hear every word.

Mom sat facing us on the sofa, her shoulders limp with exhaustion.

"Where were you?" she asked.

"We drove to Frederick," Nory said.

"Frederick?"

I didn't want it to sound as though it was only Nory's idea, as though I had just gone along for the ride.

"We went to see if we could live with Mel Kramer, but he wasn't there," I told them.

"Oh, Ted!" Mom cried, and closed her eyes.

Dad studied us as though he didn't believe it, then I could see by his face that he did.

"Whose idea was that?" he asked.

"Mine," said Nory.

"I wanted to go as much as he did," I added.

"Nory, if only you knew how *worried* we've been—almost out of our minds!" said Mom.

"How do you think we've felt all week?" Nory shot back. "All summer! The last couple *years,* in fact!"

Good going, Nory, I thought.

"Sha!" whispered Grandma, surprised. We were all surprised.

"But it's not as though we *meant* to make you worry," Mom said.

"Well, what *we* meant was to just get out of your life so you and Dad wouldn't have to argue about us," Nory told her.

Mom's chin trembled.

"I refuse to be intimidated," Dad said. "Don't think you can just run off when something goes wrong. We tried to get you to talk this over with us at breakfast. Why didn't you tell us then how you felt?"

"Because I had the breath knocked out of me, that's why," Nory yelled. "Because I felt like I'd been kicked in the stomach and sat on. Ted and I have been caught in the middle ever since you and Mom started fighting, and we're sick of it."

Grandma Rose, sitting in the background, nodded her head encouragingly.

"We're a team," I said to Mom and Dad. "Just because *you* aren't a team anymore, don't try to split *us* up."

Grandma waved one fist triumphantly in the air, but jerked her arm down quickly when Dad turned his head.

"Well, if that's how you boys feel, I'm glad you can get it out," he said, "but don't think that this afternoon is going to change anything."

"Hold your horses, Gene." It was Grandma talking. "Finally in the end we are all having a good discussion. Gene, you want to talk serious, now?"

"Mother," Mom interrupted. "I really don't think that you should—"

"Some respect, if you please," said Grandma sternly. "At my age, which is seventy plus, I am a little bit smart. I'll shut up, that's what you want, but first a point I've got to make. You ask what you should do?"

"We didn't really ask, Mother."

"Well, I tell you anyway what's good for you to know. You put Nory in one house and Ted in another and you are cutting them in two. Half a heart, that's all you'll get."

"What?" said Dad, not quite following. When Grandma gets going, sometimes, she skips the necessary details.

"*Solomon* knew. That old king was a brain and a half."

"What's she talking about?" Dad asked Mom.

"You want to see hurt?" Grandma barreled

on. "You think I don't know hurt? You divide up two boys, and all you'll get is one arm and one leg. So I'm shutting up, but what I said it's true anyway."

Dad got up and started for the phone in the hallway. "We'll talk about this when we're all a little more rational. In the meantime, I'd better call the police and tell them you boys are home."

I took my egg out into the kitchen, cracked it into a bowl, and gave it to Cleo.

It was Nory and I who drove Grandma to the Metro station Sunday night. She had her big leather purse on one arm and her shopping bag on the other, and down at her feet, the little overnight bag she always brings when she visits. I didn't realize till I was sitting there beside her just how tiny Grandma really is. She hardly comes up to my nose.

"Oh-ho," she said, remembering. "Have I got something for you! I almost forgot." She reached in her purse, rummaged around, and came up finally with two ten dollar bills. She handed one to me and stuck the other in Nory's shirt pocket because he was driving.

"That's a start on camp next summer," she said. "From the sweaters I returned, if you will kindly remember."

"Thanks, Grandma," Nory said. "It helps."

She sighed. "If you ask me (but who's asking?),

all this separate houses business is one big mistake and a half. 'Anybody got a cheer for staying together?' I said to Elaine. But she says, 'Mother, we're beyond that.' So I say, 'Elaine, try to get smart. There's trouble enough these days, and if you don't listen to me for once, I can't be responsible. Do you think I didn't ever suffer with your father—his indigestion and flat feet and some other things I don't even like to mention?' 'Mother, you're telling me to stay with Gene?' she asks. 'Darling, yes,' I said. 'Stay together.' 'No,' she says, 'it's over.' " Grandma shook her head. "Who can talk with such a daughter?"

"You tried, Grandma," I told her.

"Life goes on," she said. "Rome wasn't built in a day, and it's always the darkest before the light at the end of the tunnel."

We carried her bags as far as we could at the Metro station, but when she reached the turnstile, she kissed us both good-bye.

"It's not the end of the world," she said. "You're both stronger than you think. You don't carry the name of that old king for nothing, you know."

We watched her ride up the escalator but couldn't see the top. First her bluish-white hair disappeared, then her big black pocketbook, and finally the cuffs of her seersucker slacks. We rode home with Cleo behind us and found that

Grandma had left a little bag of Necco wafers on the seat, plus a dog biscuit for Cleo, should we get hungry before we got home. Grandma still doesn't believe you can go on a trip without starving, even if it's only a fifteen-minute ride to the Metro. (But Necco wafers, as she always says, aren't fattening.)

On Monday, Nory said we ought to get a job—earn some money for camp. In fact, we ought to get a job that took two people so that Mom and Dad *couldn't* split us up.

"Ha!" I said. "You don't go looking for a summer job in August, Nory!"

"I mean a job we can keep for a while."

"Ha!" I said again. The thing about Nory is he just isn't practical. I mean, you have to make phone calls and have people hang up on you and ask dumb questions so people will laugh at you and you have to knock on about two dozen doors and have folks say no in your face before you get a job. I rummaged around in the refrigerator while Nory looked through the want-ads.

"What about this one?" he said, coming out in the kitchen.

Newspaper carriers wanted, the ad read. *Silver Spring, Kensington, Garrett Park.* There was a number to call.

"What's so special about that one?" I asked. But Nory pointed to a line at the bottom:

Got a partner? Take a double route. Double the pay in half the time.

There was something wrong with the logic, but I just shrugged. Nory went out in the hall and dialed the number. I heard him talking with someone and then he was back in the kitchen.

"We've got an appointment," he said.

I turned around and stared. "For what?"

"To be interviewed by the distributor."

I just couldn't stand it. If *I'd* made that phone call, they would have asked to speak to my mother! But I was beginning to feel a little excited.

"What'll I wear?" I asked. I'd never been interviewed before.

"Your Adidas tee shirt's okay, but your socks are dirty," Nory said, so I changed.

I had a balony sandwich for breakfast, but Nory wouldn't let me put any onions on it. You never eat onions when you go for an interview, he said. I don't know what guys do who don't have older brothers to tell them things like that.

It felt like old times with Nory. We took a bus to Silver Spring and then walked around looking for the address. It was somebody's house with a little office just inside the front door. The distributor wore a shirt rolled up at the sleeves and had a huge pot belly. I tried not to stare at his stomach.

"So you want to work for the newspaper, huh?" he said. He gave us each a form to fill out. In the space called "place of previous employment," I didn't write anything. I kept sneaking a look at Nory's application to be sure I was doing it right.

"I got a number of routes opening up," the man said, looking through his file cards, and pulled one from the box. "Here's a long route—good for two people—just five blocks from your street. Papers are delivered at five in the morning and you have to have them on the doorstep by six-thirty or people start calling. I get a lot of complaints, I'm looking for two new carriers. You understand?"

We nodded. The distributor gave us a list of addresses where we would deliver the paper and told us to meet him at Lexington and Dupont at five o'clock the next morning. He'd run through the route with us.

"We're hired, then?" I asked. I couldn't believe we'd get it so easily.

"You're down in the books," the man said.

The alarm went off Tuesday morning at four forty-five. Nory and I both leaped out of bed and collided there in the middle, groggy with sleep. We pulled on our jeans and tee shirts and grabbed Pop Tarts to eat on the way.

It took an hour and a half to do the papers. Nory worked one side of the streets and I worked the other. The distributor told us which houses had dogs to look out for and which owners would be the first to complain if the paper was late. We got up every morning that week, and by Thursday, Cleo had her cast off and could go with us.

Dad and Mom were trying to help, we could tell. As soon as we headed for bed in the evening, Dad would turn the TV down so it wouldn't bother us. In the morning, we usually found doughnuts or rolls all ready on the counter.

"How much do you earn?" Dad asked us one night.

"About a hundred dollars a month," Nory said. "If we do okay the distributor's going to add an apartment building to our route, and that will make it a hundred twenty-five."

"Not bad," said Dad.

"I just hope it won't interfere with school," Mom said. "Five o'clock's going to seem awfully early on a cold winter morning." She was talking about winter, but her voice was warm.

The quarreling had stopped. Mom and Dad both seemed impressed by the way Nory and I got ourselves off in the morning without any help from them. I guess I was hoping they would feel they couldn't separate us now. As it turned out, though, it wasn't the job that changed their minds.

One evening, at dinner, Mom said she had an announcement to make. I wished that for just once in our house somebody would say something without an introduction first. Anyway, I stopped eating and sat there with a piece of potato in my mouth. I knew somehow that this was it—that whatever Mom and Dad had decided this time would stick. Any discussions they'd had the last few days had been quiet and serious, and they would be very sure of themselves before announcing something else. Beside me, Nory tensed.

"We've decided," Mom said, "Gene and I, that if anybody has to come home to an empty house, it should be one of us, certainly not you. So Gene is going to rent an apartment, and he and I will take turns living in it, six months or so at a time. It certainly will mean a lot of moving back and forth, but we'll each have our own special time to live here with you boys, and of course you can visit the other parent as much as you like."

How does it feel to know that your folks are finally separating, probably for good? Awful. How does it feel to know that at last the quarreling is over? Better. What's it like to know that you can go on growing up with your brother, for a while, anyway, until he marries Mickey Johnson or something? A big relief, that's what.

It wasn't what I really hoped that Mom would say, but the uncertainty, at least, was gone. For the first time in months, I was breathing easier, and I knew that Nory was, too.

"I've found an apartment on Rockville Pike," Dad said. "It's a little further than we'd like, but now that you're driving, Nory, it shouldn't be any problem for you and Ted to come over whenever you want."

"It has two bedrooms," Mom went on, "and we'll put twin beds in one so that when you're visiting you'll have a permanent place for your things."

Dad reached across the table and put one hand on my shoulder, one on Nory's. "We've been under a lot of stress these last few weeks, and sometimes when people are tired, they make some really stupid decisions."

"Yeah, I know how that is," said Nory.

We went to see the apartment after dinner—Dad and Nory and I. It was a high rise with chairs and artificial plants in the lobby and music in the elevators. Dad's apartment was on the ninth floor and overlooked the tennis court. "Pool's on the other side," he said. "You'll enjoy that, I know."

Nory and I snooped around the building and found the rooftop lounge and a sauna in the basement. It reminded me of the way we used to explore whenever we stopped at a motel on vacation. Nory and I would scout around, trying all the Coke machines for leftover change, checking out the pool to see if there was a water slide. . . . But this time it was different. Mom wasn't along. We wouldn't be sharing things like we used to, the four of us, probably not ever again. A huge lump swelled in my throat so that I couldn't talk. I went back to the lobby and waited there for Dad and Nory.

Moving day was set for Saturday. Nory was playing in a tennis match at the Y and wouldn't be home. Mom left, too. She asked Nory to drive her to the mall that morning and pick her up again at five.

"There's roast beef sandwiches when you get hungry, Ted. Okay?" she said.

"Okay." So this was the way it would be, I thought. I'd worried about the final scene between my parents—wondered what two people who had lived together for eighteen years would say just before they separated. Now I knew. They wouldn't say anything at all.

I sat on the stairs with Cleo, listening to Dad moving around the bedroom at the end of the hall. Finally I went to the doorway and said, "Need any help, Dad?"

He stopped and looked at the boxes piled on the floor. "Well, maybe so. I guess you could pack all my shoes in the zipper bag."

I was glad to have something to do. Cleo knew that things weren't right and lay in the hall, head on her paws. Her eyes looked the way I felt inside. Dad went on emptying the dresser drawers.

"There's room left over," I said when the shoes

were in. "Want me to pack the things on your closet shelf?"

"Would you? That would be fine." His voice was too cheerful. Of course it wasn't fine. Nothing was fine.

I reached up and scooped up a bunch of stuff—camera, unused tie rack, golf balls, and an old wallet that I had made for Dad the second summer I was at camp. It was really ugly. The stitching around the sides was crooked and there was a hideous leather fringe around the bottom. Most fathers would have thrown it out long ago, but Dad had kept it all these years. I just stood there, staring at the wallet, and then I heard Dad say, "Ted. . . . "

I dropped the wallet and threw my arms around him, burying my face against his shoulder. I tried to speak, but words wouldn't come—just gulp after gulp. Dad hugged me hard. He was swallowing, too.

"I wish. . . . " I said finally, but couldn't go on.

"So do I," said Dad gently.

We finished the packing and I helped carry things down to the front porch. Uncle David drove up with a U-Haul hooked onto his Cadillac. That looked as out of place as Uncle David himself. I could see some of the neighbors watching out their windows. I didn't want them watching.

"Well, well, nice weather, isn't it?" Uncle David said to me, coming up on the porch. "Could have been pouring down rain. We'll just get this little business here over with—"

"Uncle David," I said, "let's not pretend. It's not 'little business' at all."

He stared at me, then quickly began stacking boxes.

"Well . . . ," he began, but didn't know what to say, so finally he walked back to the U-Haul without answering.

Dad and I made several trips to the bedroom and den before we got everything out on the porch.

"Got your tennis racket?" Uncle David said heartily. "Going to build up that old tennis arm again, I'll bet. Nice court they've got over there."

I wondered if Uncle David would talk like that if Aunt Sheila ever left him. I bet he'd never even considered the possibility. It was scary when you realized that maybe nothing was forever.

When all of Dad's things were in the U-Haul, he said, "Remember that you're having dinner with me next Wednesday, you and Nory."

"I'll remember," I told him.

I watched him get in Uncle David's car, but just as the motor started, I remembered something.

"Dad!" I leaped down the steps and ran up to the window. "John Jennings and his father are going on a raft trip the third Saturday in September. They want us to go too—you and me. Can we?"

"White-water rafting? I'd love it," said Dad. "Tell them we'll go."

He smiled at me, and I smiled back, and I didn't even mind that Uncle David was smiling. Now that I knew I wouldn't have to go live with him, Uncle David didn't seem so bad.

Nory came home, and we made ourselves some sandwiches and ate them out on the glider. Things were the same between Nory and me again and yet they were different. It was hard to explain.

"Nory," I said, "does it ever bother you that nothing is forever?"

"Not everyone gets divorced," Nory said.

"Yeah, but . . . people change. Did you ever notice how the guys who were best friends in second grade aren't best friends anymore when they get to junior high? Or that when a bunch of guys hang around together and feel close, one of them moves away?"

I knew, somehow, that I wasn't really talking about divorce or even the guys at school. Nory knew it too.

"We've had some good times ourselves, Ted—going to camp together, riding our bikes to the pool—but would you really want to go on doing that for the rest of our lives?"

"That's so terrible?" I asked.

"It would look pretty funny when we got to be twenty-five."

"We could ride around together in a car," I said. Nory has no imagination.

"Sure," said Nory. "But we can't always stick together like a peanut butter sandwich."

I was getting the message.

"What about all our plans though, Nory? What about that camp we talked about starting some day?"

"Listen," Nory said, "all kinds of things could happen. Maybe you'll start a camp in the Catskills and call it Ted's Retreat. Maybe I'll open a restaurant in Pittsburgh. Maybe we'll run a shoe store together, you and I—Solomon Brothers Foot Apparel or something. Who knows what will happen?"

Nory's really nuts. Who would ever go to a camp called Ted's Retreat? What makes him think he could run a restaurant? He can't even make puddings. And what do either of us know about shoes?

Then I realized I didn't have to worry about all that. Maybe all I had to do—right then, anyway—was be thirteen. I didn't have to plan my whole life that afternoon, or Nory's either. Or even Mom's and Dad's. I couldn't help worrying, but I didn't have to worry all the time about everything.

I tried to think what I would like to do most at that particular moment of being thirteen.

"You know what I want to do?" I said to Nory. "Right now? Right this very minute? Take Dad a roast beef sandwich."

And we did.